The Insatiable Maw

MICK LOWE

The Insatiable Maw

A Story of Eco-Resistance

THE NICKEL RANGE TRILOGY • VOLUME 2

Baraka
Books

Montréal

ISBN 978-1-77186-037-6 pbk; 978-1-77186-044-4 epub; 978-1-77186-045-1 pdf; 978-1-77186-046-8 mobi/kindle

All illustrations including cover by Oryst Sawchuk
Cover by Folio Infographie
Book design by Folio Infographie
Legal Deposit, 2nd quarter 2015

Bibliothèque et Archives nationales du Québec
Library and Archives Canada

Published by Baraka Books of Montreal.
6977, rue Lacroix
Montréal, Québec H4E 2V4
Telephone: 514 808-8504
info@barakabooks.com
www.barakabooks.com

Printed and bound in Quebec, Canada

Société
de développement
des entreprises
culturelles
Québec

Baraka Books acknowledges the generous support of its publishing program from the Société de développement des entreprises culturelles du Québec (SODEC), the Government of Quebec, tax credit for book publishing administered by SODEC, and the Canada Council for the Arts.

Canada Council
for the Arts

We acknowledge the financial support of the Government of Canada, through the National Translation Program for Book Publishing for our translation activities and through the Canada Book Fund (CBF) for our publishing activities.

Trade Distribution & Returns
Canada and the United States
Independent Publishers Group
1-800-888-4741 (IPG1);
orders@ipgbook.com

Contents

For Homer Seguin, who kept the story alive.

Based on actual events.

PART ONE

The Insatiable Maw

1

The Return of Jake McCool

The rust-encrusted school bus braked to a screeching halt in the central yard of the Copper Cliff smelter complex. What at first appeared to be reddish rust rimming the wheel wells of the aging yellow bus would, upon closer inspection, turn out to be the fine, reddish powdery dust that clings to every surface here in ground zero of one of the world's largest, and most noxious, base-metal smelters.

Jake McCool is about to climb warily down the steps of the bus, setting foot back on company property for the first time in fully five years. Hard to believe it has been that long since the freak mining accident that ended his mining career forever.

It had not been an easy time, what with his suspension from work underground, the result of strict doctor's orders, and the years of arduous, even painful, physiotherapy sessions intended to strengthen his badly twisted back. The loss of his rich bonus earnings had proved ruinous, leading to a much-reduced lifestyle.

His beloved '57 Chevy Biscayne—his first car—had been forfeited, and he and his girlfriend Jo Ann Winter had elected to join a "commune"—a co-op house, really—that his old friend Foley Gilpin had started up in a spacious old red-brick house near downtown Sudbury. His accident had had a grievous impact on Jo Ann, too. She had refused to leave Jake while he was still convalescing in hospital, choosing not to return to her studies at Ryerson Polytechnic in downtown Toronto.

The establishment of "The Gilpin Co-op" followed a suspicious fire that had nearly killed Foley and that had burned them out of the apartment that Jake had been sharing with Jo Ann and Gilpin.

After his mining accident Jake had been forced onto Worker's Comp, which paid him only a fraction of his underground wages—minus the bonus, of course. The Ontario Workers' Compensation Board had proved a hellish bureaucracy more concerned with getting Jake, and the thousands of Sudbury workers maimed and injured at Inco each year, off their payroll and back into the workforce than it was with any kind of meaningful rehabilitation or support for the injured workers in its care.

No matter how you sliced it, Jake had learned, there was a certain stigma attached to being "on Comp," as if you were some kind of malingerer milking the system, when in fact most of his fellow claimants, like Jake himself, struggled with both chronic pain and low-level depression at the enforced idleness of being off the job, conditions that were not improved by a social status that ranked them only slightly above welfare recipients and left them in a perpetual state of rage against the all-powerful bureaucrats who ruled the WCB with absolute—and often arbitrary—authority. One year, for example, Jake and a number of his fellow Comp claimants found themselves cut off Compensation benefits altogether just before Christmas. Why does a dog lick his balls? Because he can.

And so at this moment Jake is about to enter into a new kind of Hell, in his first day as a worker at the Copper Cliff nickel smelter.

"Fellas, this here's the Number Three Dry, take your work clothes in, and change outta your street clothes." The speaker is a small officious man in crisp new overalls wearing a white hard hat. He stands at the front of the bus between the driver and the door. He has to yell slightly to make himself heard all the way to the back of the bus.

Only then does Jake become aware of the noise outside, a low, ominous roar whose source is impossible to pinpoint—like the intense smell of sulphur, like the fine dry red powdery dust, it just *is* constant and all-pervasive.

Welcome to the insatiable maw of the Copper Cliff smelter.

All around him Jake's fellow passengers are rising to their feet, identical plastic bags in hand, shuffling dutifully toward the front of the bus. Jake himself does not move. Inside the plastic bags, he knows, is the freshly-issued work clothing and safety gear assigned to each of the new hires, the price of which will be deducted from their first pay cheque. Jake is already dressed for work, attired in his miner's garb—coveralls, hardhat, and safety boots. A stranger slides into the seat next to Jake.

"Just coming over from the mines?"

"Is it that obvious?"

"Hard hat's a dead giveaway."

Jake felt the metal clip at the front of his hard hat, an appurtenance designed to mount a miner's cap lamp.

"And a Mine Miller, too, I see. Put 'er there, brother. I'm Randall McIvor." The stranger had evidently studied Jake's lunch pail, the Sudbury miner's standard-issue aluminum lunch box, plastered with the stickers that told much about a man's political pedigree—who he'd supported in the elections for Local Union President, as well as his allegiance during the recent epic inter-union battle between the Steelworkers and the Mine Mill. It was true, like his father and uncles before him, Jake was a Mine Mill supporter.

"Pleased to meet ya. I'm Jake McCool."

The two men fell into the easy banter typical of two former miners, both secretly relieved to have met someone of their own kind on the first day of their respective assignments in this new and unfamiliar workplace. Left unsaid was the mutual realization that their very presence here on the bus in the smelter yard was a considerable comedown. No hard rock miner worth his salt welcomed a transfer to a surface plant. There was no bonus pay, for one thing, and the mystique and camaraderie of a miner's life was also lacking.

Still, they were gainfully employed and drawing a very respectable hourly wage in a heavy industry vital to the North American economy, a source of considerable pride on both counts.

"So whaddaya think of our new union?"

Jake shrugged. "Well, '66 was a fuck-up, for sure. Not as bad as '58 with the old Mine Mill, maybe, but still. . ." his voice trailed off.

McIvor nodded in agreement, and both men fell silent, each wrapped in his own reminiscence of the two legendary, but ultimately futile, strikes their unions had waged against the largest nickel producing company the world had ever seen. The fact was they had been badly whipped, though they had belonged to two different unions, and the reasons for their losses had varied widely. In 1958, their first strike ever, they had badly overestimated the impact their strike would have while underestimating the company's resolve. Their union, already weakened by a decade-long running Cold War battle with the United Steelworkers Union, had run out of money for strike pay, and the proud Sudbury rank-and-file had simply been starved out, forced to return to work for the same offer the company had made before the suicidal strike began. The shame and bitterness at such resounding defeat festered, and the Mine Mill union was swept away in the recriminations that followed, voted out by the narrowest of margins after a prolonged period of raiding by the Steelworkers that became known locally simply as "The Raids," a turbulent period of rancorous inter-union strife that had seen the Steelworkers voted in

17

as the bargaining agents for the huge workforce of the International Nickel Company, but not at the Falconbridge Nickel Mines, Inco's much smaller crosstown rival. The once-mighty Mine Mill Local 598 survived, but only just—as a rump and a mere shadow of its former self.

A new trade union colossus—Local 6500 of the United Steelworkers—had emerged from the ashes, its members eager for payback for the debacle of 1958. Long-simmering rank-and-file rage had bubbled over several times, usually in the form of wildcats—illegal walkouts at an individual plant or mine. But as the contract with Inco expired in 1966 a company-wide wildcat ensued, resulting in chaos and a state of anarchy on the picket lines. When a handful of liquored-up hot heads took potshots at the helicopters the company had hired to ferry managers in and out of the strikebound smelter, the action made for sensational news nation-wide. The rounds, fired from a high-powered hunting rifle, all missed, but the prospect of thousands of heavily-armed Sudbury miners—who knew how to blow things up, after all—running amok triggered an invasion by the Ontario Provincial Police, who were dispatched to Sudbury in squadrons. They soon filled every motel room in the city, and the strikers responded by slashing the tires of their patrol cars. The squadrons of OPP soon became whole platoons.

The picket lines were also beyond the union's control, as one Local Union leader dispatched to the Frood Mine plant gate to restore order quickly discovered. Soon after his arrival he found himself staring death in the face when an angry picketer jumped into his car and began gunning it back and forth, vowing to run down any man who interfered with the picket line.

Homicide was averted when a lone picketer calmly stepped between the roaring vehicle and the union officer. But the damage was done. The company fired strikers wholesale as punishment for their participation in what was, in fact, an illegal strike. The union was forced to negotiate to win the employees back, foregoing other valuable union gains in the process. The resulting contract left much on the table, which did little to appease the widespread rank-and-file bitterness—toward both the union and the company—that was fast becoming bred in the bone.

"Wonder if we've learned anything since '66?" Jake mused aloud.

This time it was McIvor's turn to shrug. "I dunno—guess we'll find out next year." The impending round of bargaining was something they were all looking forward to. Nickel prices were sky high, thanks to the Vietnam War, in which the Americans were becoming ever more deeply embroiled. The U.S. had no nickel deposits of its own, but depended heavily on Sudbury as a source for this militarily vital commodity, which had fuelled a decade-long boom for the Canadian nickel capital. Neither of these facts was lost on the Sudbury rank-and-file, or on McCool and McIvor as they awaited the return of their fellow workers from the Number Three Dry.

At last, the new smelter hires clambered back onto the bus.

And the white hat, who had been impatiently tapping his clipboard with his ballpoint, once again rose to his feet. "Okay now, fellas, we're gonna start you out with a basic tour of the Copper Cliff Smelter Complex." He nodded to the driver, and the bus ground into gear.

"First stop," yelled the tour guide, checking his wristwatch, "is the furnaces which are really the heart of the whole Smelter Complex!" The bus wended along a narrow, maze-like roadway between towering buildings with sides several stories high. Their curtain walls were clad in nondescript aging red brick. After travelling for some time within what Jake was beginning to realize was a truly vast industrial complex—a city within a city, really—the bus braked to another screeching halt. This time, as everyone trooped off the bus, Jake and Randall joined the mass exodus. They entered one of the brick buildings through an open door so large it resembled the entrance to an aircraft hangar.

The rotten egg reek of sulphur became as intense as Jake had ever experienced. The crew from the bus were enveloped in a cloud of the stuff so dense it made their eyes water.

Yet somehow their tour guide seemed oblivious to the gas, noise and stink that assaulted all their senses so unpleasantly in an almost nauseating rush. Instead, he beamed at them with an expression that conjured almost filial pride and affection.

"Okay, fellas, I see we're just in time to witness something very, very special. It's a sight you don't see every day and that very few Canadians have ever seen, at all—the tapping of a furnace here at the Copper Cliff Smelter." He gestured toward an imposing wall several stories tall lined with a bewildering array of pipes and hoses. Eventually a solitary figure, garbed in a long, reflective silver robe and wearing a spaceman-style helmet approached the wall. In addition to the helmet, his face was further protected by the kind of heavy visor Jake had seen welders use.

The heavily protected figure carried a long metal rod, which he began to poke into the wall. It seemed an impossible quest at first—one human being probing, and by hand, yet!—an apparently impregnable wall several times his own height. But he seemed to know what he was about, and finally an impossibly bright light gleamed through the smallest aperture in the wall. At this point a second figure emerged, running onto the scene, bearing a heavy metal shield nearly as tall as he was. He interposed himself between the probing worker with the long pole and the wall.

The initial figure, meanwhile, had continued to twist the end of his probe around the tiny breach he'd created, opening a fissure wide enough to allow a flow of liquid the likes of which Jake had never seen—or, at least, not up this close.

The spectacle of the molten liquid flowing like lava was breathtaking in its intensity—at once too hot and bright to look directly at, and yet too dazzling to ignore.

Jake was reminded of a night long ago, when he and his girlfriend Jo Ann had parked beneath the slag heaps that flanked the smelter to make out while watching the pouring of the slag, a standard weekend Sudbury ritual for amorous couples. "So is that the slag, then?" Jake addressed his question to their tour guide, who had positioned himself at Jake's elbow for some reason.

"No, sir! That's the good stuff—what we call matte." White Hat pitched his voice below the smelter's roar, so he could speak into Jake's ear with something approaching a normal speaking level.

Jake nodded. Of course. The molten stuff was being carefully collected into some kind of ladle, he could see that now, which would not seem to be the case with slag.

"The furnace separates the matte from the slag— the matte floats to the top and the heavier slag sinks to the bottom," the White Hat explained. "An experienced furnace operator learns to distinguish one from the other while he's tapping just by watching the flow. The matte is still only about six per cent pure, though. But that's still much better than when it arrived from the mill as concentrate."

Jake nodded again. This much he understood. The point of the entire procedure with its titanic technology and almost otherworldly alchemy was to remove impurities from the sulphur-laced muck he blasted out of the mine and to extrude only the purest metals—nickel, most of all, but also copper and cobalt, and even precious metals—gold, silver and platinum.

"All right, everyone. Let's get back on the bus and go visit the next stage in the process—matte processing."

Once they had resumed their seats, Mr. White Hat turned to face them once again. As subtly as he could he cleared his throat before speaking, which Jake took as the slightest sign that even he, the ever-crisp, ever-smiling White Hat was not quite as oblivious to the smelter fumes, gas and dust as he let on. Jake's own nostrils, lungs and chest felt packed with the nasty stuff. The sounds of coughing and throat clearing could now be heard throughout the bus. "Okay, fellas next we'll see where the smelter matte goes after it leaves the Furnace Department—to Matte Processing, and the converter aisles."

Again the bus wound a bewildering course between grimy red-brick buildings, all of which looked the same to Jake. After a briefer passage it stopped, and they all shuffled dutifully off behind White Hat, still toting his clipboard. As they were about to enter another building he turned to face them. "This is where the smelter matte comes for further reduction to remove still more impurities—the converter aisle. The converter aisles of the Copper Cliff smelter are the longest converter aisles in the world, by the way." He spoke with an unmistakable pride, and turned to lead them into the building.

They entered a vast structure, the size of several football fields placed end to end. What was even more impressive was the height of the ceiling, which could not, in fact, be seen at all. It was obscured by gas and dust, but beneath it, suspended from rails, a steady stream of hot metal ladles passed over head, each accompanied by the wailing of a warning siren that left no doubt that certain death was passing by, suspended high above their heads. This was, Jake decided, the most hellish place he'd seen yet.

"Well, that's it!" announced a member of Jake's little party. "I ain't workin' here!" His voice conveyed a combination of desperation and defiance, and with that he spun around and headed for the door. The speaker had a full beard and longish hair—clearly a devotee of the hippy look. Few of Jake's friends could truly be described as hippies, though Jake himself had begun sporting a moustache and his hair was approaching collar-length, and his girlfriend Jo Ann was fond of floor-length denim skirts and wore her pretty brunette hair long, and parted straight down the middle.

"Hey!" sputtered White Hat, seemingly fazed for the first time that day. "You haven't paid for your boots yet!"

The raw recruit stopped dead in his tracks, looking down at his boots and then at White Hat. In an instant he bent down to untie the laces on his brand new work boots, which he removed one at a time while hopping awkwardly on one leg. "Here!" He handed the boots to the astonished Mr. White Hat, turned, and in his stocking feet strode defiantly out of the building. Not for the last time, a part of Jake wished he'd gone with him.

2

A Call in the Night

Harry Wardell got the call late at night on the eve of his maiden speech in the Ontario Legislature. The newly-elected Member of the Provincial Parliament for Sudbury was comfortably ensconced, wearing his slippers and pyjamas, in his newly-rented apartment in downtown Toronto, a short walk away from the Legislature buildings in Queen's Park. He was sitting with his feet up on the coffee table, contemplating that first speech—or was it to be simply a question during Question Period?—when the ringing telephone suddenly pierced the quiet of his rooms, scattering his thoughts about the morrow, but answering his questions, too.

The caller was one of Wardell's prime sources of information about Inco, the huge nickel company that dominated affairs in his hometown. It operated on such a colossal scale that, like the mythical Colossus of Rhodes, it dwarfed everyone around it.

"Yes?" Wardell began.

"Listen, Harry, there's something going on up here I think you should know about."

"Yes?" Wardell repeated. "Go ahead, I'm listening."

"There's something going on at the smelter. The boys tell me they've got them in there workin' around the clock, cleaning up. Word is there's to be an inspection. . ."

"Let me guess: the inspectors have very kindly called ahead to warn the company, as usual."

"That's about the size of it, yes."

This *was* useful information, and Wardell had no doubts as to its veracity. His caller was a health and safety activist with the United Steelworkers of America, whose Local 6500 represented production and maintenance workers at the sprawling nickel company. His informant's tips had always proved spot-on in the past, and this latest heads-up was just the latest indication of the cozy relationship that existed between the nickel giant and the government that was supposed to regulate it on behalf of his constituents. Useful, even explosive, information, but somehow he had to turn it into more than just water cooler gossip at the Steel Hall in the morning. He needed a paper trail, some form of documentary evidence. . . Wardell's mind went into overdrive, and then he had it. Suddenly he pulled his long, lean frame upright. His slippers hit the floor. "Listen, Paul, I need you to put this in a telegram. Go downtown to the CPR telegraph office right away and send me a telegram containing this information, but for God's sake make sure there's today's date on the thing. Got that?"

Wardell repeated his instructions. There was no mistaking the urgency in his voice.

"Okay, Harry, okay. Keep your shirt on. I'm on my way downtown right now."

And with that the caller hung up abruptly, and Wardell, excited now, began pacing the room, which suddenly seemed much too small for his six-foot-six frame.

His debut in the House tomorrow would be a question, and now he knew just what that question would be. Even better, he already knew the answer.

Jake flopped down wearily on the living room couch, which, like most of the rest of the furniture in the house, had just been purchased at the Sally Ann. His ears were ringing and he had the intense desire to clear his nostrils and lungs of the reek of sulphur, which at times that first day had been so strong he'd had to struggle to suppress successive waves of nausea.

"Well, how'd it go?" Foley Gilpin asked.

Jake, his head lolling back on the back of the couch, wagged it from side to side. The thought that he had to return to the smelter in a little over eight hours was almost more than he could bear.

"Awful. Just awful. The gas in there, the dust, the noise. . ."

"It's an absolute hell hole." Jake was staring up at the high ceiling of the old house as he said this, too weary and disconsolate to even look his friend in the eye.

At least there was this—his friendship with Foley, and the refuge this house had become. Theirs was an unlikely friendship; they were years apart in age, and their backgrounds were also worlds apart. Gilpin was much older, and there was a vaguely bohemian air about the bespectacled, slightly portly reporter, an air he was happily cultivating by letting what little hair he had grow long. Even though he was older than most of the downtown Sudbury crowd they hung out with, Foley was clearly ready to channel his inner hippy, embracing the Aquarian Age with open arms, a true free spirit. A native of Chicago and a newspaperman by trade, Foley also possessed a certain world-weariness, a worldly air of sophistication that Jake, the scion of a Sudbury working-class family, totally lacked.

Jake had lived his whole life in Sudbury, rarely venturing further afield than Toronto. He'd never been west of Wawa. The idea of freelancing for a living, living by his wits as Foley was now doing, was unimaginable. For Jake toting a lunch bucket each day to work for Mother Inco was part of his DNA.

They were poles apart when it came to education, too. Gilpin was a graduate of the Medill School of Journalism at Chicago's Northwestern University, while Jake was a grade ten dropout.

But despite all the outward differences they had an unbreakable bond of friendship that had been forged during the recent Mine Mill-Steel raids. They'd both fought on the Mine Mill side—Foley with his writing, Jake with his fists.

And they shared something else: a bizarre mid-morning encounter on the top floor of the President Hotel downtown, where they'd gone in search of a mysterious, malevolent figure who had killed Jake's brother

Ben in a late night alleyway encounter behind the Coulson Hotel. They found their quarry, of that Jake was certain. But with him in his room they'd also found Jo Ann's dad, a startling revelation that had sent Jake reeling from the room. It was a unique experience that only the two of them shared—to this day Jake had never disclosed the matter to Jo Ann—he'd no idea how to broach the subject with her, and, in any event the loss of his brother, and whatever role Jo Ann's father might have played in his brother's brutal murder was a place still too fraught with emotion to venture into. It was all a tangled web that might never be unravelled, as Mr. Winter had himself become the victim of a fatal downtown traffic accident a year later.

Gilpin listened in sympathetic silence to his young friend's plight. "Yeah, Jake," he replied at last, "the sulphur was really bad downtown today. . . I can't imagine what it must be like at ground zero. . . Listen, if ever there's anything I can do to help. . ."

"Yeah, thanks Foley, I appreciate that." Though such a thing appeared highly unlikely to Jake. The sulphur was in the ore, after all. Its presence was a permanent fixture of life in Sudbury. What could a scribbler do against such an obvious, immutable fact of life?

Jake was just beginning to feel human again when Jo Ann arrived home after her own day on the job. As always, her presence cheered Jake up immensely. She, too, listened in silence to Jake's description of conditions at the Copper Cliff smelter, except that she sat beside him on the couch, resting her head on his shoulder.

Jo Ann remained silent for a few minutes after Jake finished his account of his first day back at work. Then she snuggled up close to whisper in his ear: "Wanna go upstairs and puff one?"

Jake pulled back from her so he could look directly into her green eyes, which had lost none of their mischievous sparkle. The question required only the briefest consideration. "Sure."

The couple headed for the stairs, while Gilpin headed for the kitchen. It was his night to cook, a duty each resident shared on a rotating basis. Nightly meals involving all residents and visiting friends of residents were part of the co-op's daily routine. They lent the house a familial sense, and an opportunity for gossip and small talk everyone enjoyed.

Within moments Jake, enveloped in the pleasant smells of Foley's cooking and Jo Ann's dope, began to feel life just might be worth living again.

Jo Ann lit the joint and managed to ask a question while inhaling deeply. "So what are you gonna do, Sparky?"

Jake contemplated the joint she had just passed him. "What, about the smelter, you mean? I'm not sure there's much any of us *can* do. . . That sulphur's been a hassle since mining first started. My dad was partnered up with this old, old guy when he started working underground, and he told my dad he could even remember the days of the open bed roasters, when they'd just pile the muck in a big pit in the ground, stack in some cordwood, and set the whole pit on fire. One of the biggest roasters was in Copper Cliff, right where the park is today. This old guy said the smoke was so bad the workers' wives used to have to stand in their doorways and holler out their husbands' names up there in Little Italy, up there on the hill in behind where the smelter is now, just so their husbands could find their way home through the smoke . . . Imagine!" As it usually did, the dope had loosened Jake's tongue. This was one of the things Jo Ann loved about getting high with Jake—it got him talking.

"So what did the people back then do about it?"

"Oh, they knew it was making them sick, all right, but the company claimed there was no other way. . ."

"By which they meant no other cheaper way. . ."

"Right. So this went on for decades, and the sulphur smoke eventually killed every tree around for miles, every shrub, and every blade of grass, and that's how we ended up with all this black rock sticking up everywhere you look." The city, as they both knew it, was notorious across Canada for its harshly barren "lunar landscape."

"But *something* changed things in the end, though, right, Jake?" she passed him back the joint, and pressed the point.

"Yeah, I guess the pressure built up until the provincial government forced the company to build the smelter. . . 'Course, that wasn't 'til the Thirties."

"So you don't think history could repeat itself?"

Jake sighed, exasperated. "Honestly, Jo, I don't see how. The company's got this government in its pocket; everybody knows that. Practically owns 'em, in fact." It was the same old story: the rich and the powerful controlled everything. Jake had few illusions about the difficulty of effecting genuine change. He had, after all, fought on the losing side of the Mine Mill-Steel battle, a defeat that taught a cautionary lesson about the fight for social change and that still left a bad taste in his mouth. The good guys did not always win in the end.

Jo Ann took another hit from the joint. "So they are so big, we are so small, stay as we are. That's your conclusion? C'mon there Sparky, you can do better'n that!"

If he hadn't been so stoned, Jake might have begun to lose his temper at his girlfriend's repeated, insistent jibes, but as it was, it all just made his head spin, and he fell into a silent, stony reverie. . .

3

On the Bull Gang

The euphoria of the night before gave way to harsh reality the next morning as Jake approached the environs of the Copper Cliff smelter once more. Located just a few miles west of Sudbury proper, the smelter complex was surrounded by a wide expanse of black rock, a lifeless no-man's land that served notice that this was a place of almost superhuman toxicity. In fact, the burn created by the smelter's fumes was sufficiently large that it could be seen from space, in LANDSAT photos beamed back to Earth from orbiting satellites.

Jake's heart sank as he neared the sprawling old red-brick buildings topped by the smokestacks belching out sulphur gas that would soon be tasted and swallowed by shoppers on the streets of downtown Sudbury, five miles or so to the east.

Jake was in the dry changing out of his street clothes when he was approached by his new acquaintance of the day before, Randall McIvor. "Hey, Jake," McIvor began casually enough as he slid onto the bench next to Jake. But then he lowered his voice. "Listen, I've met somebody—he was a Mine Miller, too, so I trust him—who says he'll show us the ropes here, teach us a few things Mr. White Hat failed to mention. You interested?"

Jake shrugged. "Sure, count me in."

"D'ja get your work assignment yet?"

Jake nodded. "Yeah. Something called the bull gang." He understood it to mean a group of common labourers who were not assigned to any one place in the smelter complex, but instead "floated" to wherever they were needed.

McIvor nodded at the news. "Good! Me, too!" He stood up. "Okay then, I'll introduce you to this guy first chance we get. See ya later, Jake."

There were, in fact, a dozen bull gangs, as Jake learned when he reported for work. Each gang was made up of fifteen or so men. It was heavy, labour-intensive work, cleaning up any mess, any spill that might occur under a conveyor belt. Pure grunt work, shovelling up messes for a solid eight hours a day. To Jake a strong back and a weak mind seemed the prime requisites for the job. There were only two redeeming factors that Jake could see: as floating work parties they moved from place to place throughout the vast smelter complex, and it was interesting to experience so many different workplaces. The other highlight was that, purely through the luck of the draw, Jake was assigned to the same gang as McIvor. On their third day on the job together McIvor made good on his promise to Jake.

4

Haywire

McIvor steered Jake toward the lunch room, logic-
ally the only place where a pair of raw smelter recruits
could have a quiet discussion with a smelter veteran—and well-known union militant—away from
the prying eyes of company supervision. Already
seated at the long lunchroom table was a solitary figure in a black t-shirt. McIvor nodded at the stranger
as they sat down, and Jake found himself face-to-face
with one of the most striking—and startling—coun-
tenances he'd ever come across.

"Robert d'Aguire, this is Jake McCool," McIvor
announced.

The stranger extended a burly forearm to Jake.
"McCool? Big Bill? Walt and Bud McCool? *That*
McCool?"

"My dad and uncles," Jake affirmed.

The confirmation elicited an admiring grunt, and
d'Aguire's hand, which had twisted into a thumbs-up
handshake, squeezed even tighter in a vice-like grip.
It was all Jake could do to keep from wincing.

"Bob d'Aguire, rhymes with Haywire. Knew your dad and uncles back in the Mine Mill days... Stand-up guys, all of 'em."

"Bob here's a steward in the converter building," Randall explained.

Jake studied the man across from him. His head was shaved bald, but a long, wispy beard adorned his chin, and Jake noticed the words "Coffin Wheelers MC" tattooed on one bulging bicep.

"What's your stencil, brother?" inquired Jake, curious to know exactly what role the big biker played in the production cycle in the converters.

"Crane operator," was all d'Aguire said by way of reply.

Jake had to think about that for a minute. He had, after all, noticed no conventional cranes during his brief tour of the converter aisles. But those massive ladles of hot metal passing overhead had to have been moved somehow...

" ... so overhead crane, then?"

"Yessir."

Jake gave out a low whistle, impressed. "Man, the gas must be some bad up there."

D'Aguire merely shrugged, and nodded. "They give you a mask."

Just the thought of the gassy, congested converter aisles with the ladles of hot metal passing overhead accompanied by the banshee wail of warning sirens made Jake shudder. "Does it work?"

D'Aguire shrugged again. "Most of the time."

"Look, what I just don't get about this place is how it can even be *legal*, I mean there oughta be a law..." Jake's voice trailed off in bewilderment.

"Oh there's a law," replied d'Aguire, his voice dripping with sarcasm. "It's just that the people who enforce the law are *here*," he raised a forefinger in the air, "and the company that owns this shithole is *here*," he jabbed his middle finger into the air for emphasis. D'Aguire's dark eyes flashed with a degree of hostility that Jake found both fascinating and intimidating. He seemed the most intense person Jake had ever met. Intense, but not likeable. With his bald head and outlaw biker mien, d'Aguire projected an "I don't give a fuck" attitude that made him appear both single-minded and fearless. Jake was glad they were on the same side.

"So there *are* laws, but they just aren't enforced by anyone?"

The question elicited a peremptory grunt from d'Aguire.

"You just don't get it. Colonel Sanders runs this henhouse. Company's got about a million ways to cover its ass while it breaks the law, starting with the fact the Ministry calls over to warn the company in advance any time they're about to do an inspection. Watch graveyard shift. Any time guys are called in to work overtime on graveyards you know there's an inspection coming the next day."

"Oh, man. So we are well and truly fucked."

D'Aguire raised a cautionary hand. "Yes and no. Some of us are trying to figure a way to fight back—that's why I wanted to talk to you young fellers."

Jake nodded. He was all ears. And with that d'Aguire lowered his voice and began speaking with quiet intensity. . .

5

A Very Bad Day

There were bad days in the smelter, Jake was learning, and then there were very bad days in the smelter when things went sideways faster and much worse than anything he'd ever experienced underground. A day in the first week of his second month there was one of the latter.

It started when Jake's gang was summoned to clean up a hot metal spill in the furnace building. Such cataclysmic events were rare, but they happened.

The gang was called out to clean up the spill, which was still cooling when they arrived. A crust, or "blister" was still forming over the spill, which had pooled over much of the floor of the furnace building. There was nothing the gang could do but watch and wait, until the molten puddle solidified and they could begin their laborious task of cracking, prying and shovelling up the mess. As they were waiting Jake saw a foreman beckon to a furnace section worker Jake didn't know. Although he couldn't hear the conversation, Jake could tell the worker was being ordered to fetch something from the other side of the building. Jake watched as the worker surveyed the distance he would have to cross if he attempted a shortcut over the blister, compared to the distance around the spill. Jake had an uneasy feeling in the pit of his stomach, but he couldn't take his eyes off the worker, anonymous though he was in his nondescript coveralls and safety glasses.

The worker tested the crust of the blister with the toe of his work boot. It held. Jake held his breath as the lone figure ventured gingerly out onto the crust, like a man attempting to walk across a frozen pond after it has just iced over. At first the short cut appeared to be a good idea, but after several steps the crust began to crack, and the molten metal beneath began to bubble through. Here the worker made a fatal mistake: he began to run. His footfalls became heavier, and now every time his boots hit the crust it gave way.

Like his comrades on the bull gang, Jake watched, mesmerized by what happened next. The running man began to shrink before their horrified gaze. The molten metal melted first his boots, then his feet and then his legs. He began to founder, and fell face down. Shrieking in pain, he lay sprawled atop the crust, which supported his newly distributed weight. They all sat transfixed, as if watching a horror movie—but this was no movie.

Jake turned to the supervisor who had ordered the man to fetch. . . whatever, but the boss seemed paralyzed by the scene and was clearly flustered.

Jake's gaze returned to the injured worker, obviously in tremendous pain, isolated out on the blister.

"Somebody bring me a ladder!" Jake demanded of no one in particular, and a long aluminum ladder suddenly appeared. Jake hastily extended it to its fullest length before laying it gently over the molten puddle in the direction of his injured co-worker.

Then Jake, on all fours now, began to crawl cautiously out on the ladder toward the downed furnace worker. He could feel the intense heat radiating off the nearly still-molten spill, but the ladder distributed Jake's weight sufficiently that the crust held. The ladder was just long enough that Jake was just able to reach the injured man from the top—and last—rung. Jake reached out and clamped his wrist with his right hand. "Okay!" Jake shouted to the members of the bull gang, "Pull us back!"

The crew reefed on the foot of the ladder, and soon all three—Jake, the injured man, and the ladder, were restored to the relative safety of the smelter floor. Jake heaved a sigh of relief to be standing once again on solid ground, and he was surprised to discover that his hands and legs were shaking uncontrollably. Abashed by his own hyper-adrenalized reaction, Jake began to pace in circles, both in an effort to conceal his condition from his workmates, and to walk off and to restore his own shattered nerves.

Robert "Haywire" d'Aguire, meanwhile, was oblivious to the drama playing out in the furnace building. Perched high above the floor of the converter aisle in his overhead crane, the burly biker had problems of his own—the gas was as bad as he'd ever experienced in his years working in the converters. The problem, he knew, was with the Number Three converter. Whenever it was running the gas was almost unbearable. His gas mask was really nothing more than a cotton cloth soaked in glycerine and then dusted with baking soda—but it worked, except that it covered only his nose and mouth, leaving his eyes exposed. The gas burned his eyes, and they welled with so many tears that Haywire was soon effectively blinded. No matter how many times he wiped the tears from his eyes, they just wouldn't work in the intense gas cloud. Fuck this. With tears streaming from his eyes and his nose running inside his mask, d'Aguire could no longer do his job, at least not safely. He was moving thousands of pounds of molten material around over the heads of dozens of co-workers down there on the floor. Although he couldn't actually see them through the gas, d'Aguire knew they were down there, and he also knew that one mistaken move on his part could mean raining down certain death upon them. No, fuck it. This ladle would be his last.

After delivering the ladle to its appointed destination d'Aguire returned his crane to its starting point and then reached for the phone that connected him to the convertor supervision office, a glass-enclosed cubicle so far below him that it might as well have been on Mars. "Listen, the goddamned gas is so thick up here I can no longer operate safely," he growled into the phone. "I want a Drager and a shifter up here right away!" A disembodied voice on the other end of the line agreed meekly with d'Aguire's demands. The biker then sat motionless in his seat and waited, knowing his inactivity would not go unnoticed from below. He also expected that his mention of a Drager, the device used to monitor the level of contaminants in ambient air, would raise red flags in the supervisor's office down below. And he further expected the company's minions would take immediate steps to cover the company's ass. So, he waited. And waited. A good twenty minutes elapsed, and still no supervisor, and still no Drager meter. Also what he had expected. Though he couldn't see it, Haywire knew what was happening around him: the Number Three converter was being shut down, and every window, stack and vent in the building was being opened to clear out the gas before the supervisor arrived to take the air quality test he'd demanded.

Eventually the gas began to clear enough so that he could see someone wearing a white hat clambering up the ladder that was the only approach to his aerie high above the converter aisle. He had a Drager, d'Aguire noted, but no gas mask. The latter omission elicited first a bemused grunt from the crane operator, followed by a grim smile. Very well then. Two could play this game. . .

D'Aguire welcomed the shifter into his cab, but he could clearly see the man's unease. Whether it was the dizzying height, or the cramped space inside the crane's control room, or his forced closeness to a burly, nasty, bearded shop steward nick-named Haywire, d'Aguire could not tell, but he could see quite clearly that his new guest had arrived short of breath from the climb, and that he was perspiring heavily. His welcome consisted of a peremptory grunt from his union adversary, and a nod at the Drager.

"Know how to use that thing?"

The new arrival's white hat bobbed on his head in unison with his Adam's apple as he swallowed heavily. "Yes."

D'Aguire watched closely as the shift boss began to take the air sample. The Drager could test for nearly a dozen contaminants, depending on the glass vial inserted in the machine before the air sample was drawn. D'Aguire guessed the shifter had inserted the vial for sulphur. The testing was activated by squeezing ten times—exactly ten—on the kind of rubberized bulb that always reminded d'Aguire of a turkey baster. The union steward carefully counted the squeezes on the Drager's air pump while the white hat was absorbed in the same thing. When he had finished he paused, and the two men looked at each other.

And then, as if by mutual consent, came the moment of truth: the glass tube was carefully removed from its nest inside the device, and read. Mr. White Hat held it up so d'Aguire could see. Small black lines were painted on the side of the clear glass to measure gradations, and some kind of gas inside the tube would discolour in proportion to the impurity being measured, a form and process not dissimilar to a mercury thermometer. White Hat grinned broadly at the Drager tube he held between his fingers: the sulphur gas content had barely registered, indicating a reading of zero gas in the air. "There, see? Nothing to worry about!"

But d'Aguire only glowered at the tube, and at the shifter. "Zero," he agreed grudgingly. "That's what I want to work in *all the time*. Not a one, not a two. A zero."

The shifter, still grinning, nodded agreeably, relief clearly evident in his demeanour. Now he could be the bearer of good news to his superiors. Union complaints of unsafe and unhealthy working conditions were highly exaggerated. Science didn't lie, and he held the indisputable proof between the tips of his thumb and forefinger. Even the fearsome d'Aguire had had to agree.

The shop steward had already turned his attention to the controls of his crane, which he was running out on its rail to pick up his next payload, a ladle full of glowing, red-hot molten liquid. Hovering over the pot, he played out the wire rope, weighted by the heavy iron grapple at its end. Seemingly without effort he looped the hook into the liftpoint of the ladle, and began the heavy lift, which set off the shriek of sirens up and down the great length of the converter aisle. Within seconds the Converter Building Supervisor, observing with satisfaction d'Aguire's crane once again in motion, gave the order to re-start the Number Three converter, which represented a significant fraction of the massive building's total output. Like everyone else in the densely layered hierarchy of the company, he was measured strictly on the basis of throughput, and he could not allow an important cog in the machinery of production to remain idle a split second longer than was absolutely necessary.

At first, the return of Number Three to the line was not readily apparent in Haywire's cab. But the bearded shop steward, who with his gas mask covering his nose and mouth now resembled a bank robber from the Wild West, was not surprised by the approach of the toxic fumes.

His guest, however, was caught unawares, and unprepared. The first warning of impending disaster was nothing much—a small tickle in the back of his throat, and an odd, not entirely pleasant taste in his mouth. Not so bad. The instinctive reaction was always the same: to swallow, as if to clear the mouth of the taste, which became much more unpleasant the longer it lingered. And then there was the smell— the overpowering stench of rotten eggs. The instinctive reaction here was to hold one's breath—a futile and wholly unsustainable stratagem against a vast gaseous quantity of a mephitic *thing* that was suddenly being released after having lain dormant and undisturbed deep in the iron ribs of the Nickel Range for eons. Fearing that his lungs would burst at the losing effort, d'Aguire's guest let the last air from his lungs escape with a *whoosh!* that left him gasping for breath, and it was game over. He sucked down great gouts of the foul air and his lungs, nose and throat suddenly recoiled at the unfamiliar abuse. And so the visitor began to cough and choke, while d'Aguire sat smugly at his controls, inured by experience to the conditions, and protected, to a degree, by his face mask.

The company man began to cough and choke, struggling unsuccessfully to regain control over his breathing. He was able to stop coughing for only the briefest intervals, during which he took the shallowest, most tentative of breaths, but even those attempts meant inhaling the reeking stench of sulphur which soon overcame him once again, triggering another spasm of coughing, each round more violent than the last. He looked around himself, and at d'Aguire, who was nonchalantly operating his crane, and realized he was well and truly trapped. His only means of escape from the crane cab, and from the gas that rose to the rafters in a smothering fog so dense he could almost chew it, was the fixed steel ladder by which he had come up. But the ladder could only be accessed from the crane's stationary starting point, which D"Aquire, despite his watering eyes, now seemed to be steadfastly and studiously avoiding in order to maintain production.

Both men knew full well that the visitor had now become a hostage. The company man looked longingly at the small staging which would allow him to leave this hellish place, but d'Aguire was all business now, even though his eyes had begun to water once again, and he saw little need to return his crane to its starting point. In the meantime his guest had begun coughing once again, this time in great, gasping seizures that turned his face beet red. It was an awful sound, but d'Aguire ignored it. Finally, though, he had had enough, and he returned the crane to its staging. He gestured brusquely for the company man to be gone. "Just be careful out there," d'Aguire offered in mock solicitude. "They say the gas out there is murder."

The company man, already scrambling to get away from d'Aguire and the gas, nodded mutely, which set off another paroxysm of wheezing and gasping. And then he was gone.

As d'Aguire ran the crane back out on the rail for his next lift, he guessed that the company guy's trumpeting of the Drager reading to his superiors might now be somewhat tempered—once he was able to stop gagging long enough to form a complete sentence. D'Aguire shrugged, and went on about his business.

"*Tabernac!*" was the reaction from a member of his crew as Jake and the gang entered the converter aisle even as d'Aquire's erstwhile guest, between paroxysms of coughing, descended the fixed ladder from the rafters of the converter building.

Jake shared the cursed assessment of his French co-worker. This place was *bad,* just as gassy and dusty as he remembered from his first day orientation.

"Well, pitter patter guys, let's get at 'er," was Jake's only comment. The sooner their work here was done the sooner they could all get out of this hellish place. The remark was intended as an exhortation to his fellow members on the bull gang who, Jake sensed, had begun to look up to him as some kind of leader after his quick-thinking, purely instinctive reaction to the horrible accident that they had all just witnessed on the floor of the furnace building.

They had just begun work on the task at hand when they were distracted by yet another adverse reaction to the terrible air conditions. A worker none of them knew—a converter building regular, presumably—began to sneeze repeatedly. He was soon overcome by the fumes and began to cough uncontrollably. His body was racked by the coughing spasms, none of which sufficed to clear his nose, mouth and chest of the sulphuric tickle that afflicted them. The worker continued to cough, sputter and gasp until his face was flaming crimson and his weeping eyes were bloodshot. He dropped to his knees still retching when, before Jake's horrified gaze he began to bleed from the nose and mouth. The only thing for it, Jake decided, was to get the man out of the building. The smelter yard was a filthy, dusty place, God knew, but the conditions were at least better than in here. He motioned to McIvor for assistance, and between them they were able to lift the sputtering fellow to his feet and half-drag and half-walk him out of the building.

They left him in the yard and returned indoors, and then, without warning, Jake snapped. His arms and legs stiffened, and Jake's hands were suddenly balled into fists. Before either he or McIvor quite knew what was happening, Jake was charging at the first white hat he could find, like a dangerous rogue bull.

"Look, this is bullshit!" he screamed, spittle flying in the face of the startled white hat. "No one should have to work in this shit!" He cocked his right fist behind his ear, clearly ready to haul off and hit the defenseless boss.

"Jake! No! What the fuck?" McIvor saved the day— and likely Jake's job—by hastily grabbing Jake from behind. At some level even Jake, who was hyperventilating, knew he was on the dangerous verge of losing everything. Instead of delivering the blow he twisted free of McIvor's grasp and began to pace in circles like a man possessed, his hands opening and closing, flexing in and out of fists of their own manic, reflexive accord. None of this was lost on the other members of the bull gang who had, to a man, stopped whatever they were doing to watch Jake's meltdown with jaw-dropping amazement as the impromptu workplace drama unfolded.

Eventually Jake walked off his adrenalized state and his breathing returned to normal, although thoughts were still racing through his brain. Sure he had overreacted, but just as surely the events of this day could not stand. Jo Ann was right: somehow conditions in the smelter had to be made to change. But decking a shifter was not a winning strategy. As rage gave way to reason and he returned gradually to his senses Jake's first thought was to speak to McIvor, and he approached his best friend on the bull gang, hand extended. "Thanks there, buddy, thanks a lot. I don't know what happened to me . . . It's just no one should ever have to put up with this shit!"

McIvor nodded his head in agreement, and lowered his voice as he shook Jake's hand.

"I know, Jake, I know. Fuckin' A! But we gotta think, gotta outsmart these bastards. I'll set up a sit-down with d'Aguire."

In the event, Jake's rescue in the furnace, which was soon after described as "heroic" by the company's Public Affairs department and the local news media, was unavailing. The incident itself—the sight of a man melting from the knees down—soon entered local lore, becoming a kind of urban myth, partly because of its gruesome nature and partly because there were so many witnesses to it.

But the man Jake had rescued died a few days later in hospital. His was an agonizing, lingering death. Like so many second- and third-degree burn victims, he succumbed, eventually, to infection. The man who took the fatal shortcut would not be remembered by name, but rather for the image of a shrinking man running for his life, just one more blood sacrifice to the insatiable maw of the Copper Cliff smelter.

United Steelworkers Hall before the fire, 92 Frood Road

PART TWO-

Arms to Parley

6

Sudbury Goes to Queen's Park

Harry Wardell strode confidently, even eagerly, toward the doors of the legislative assembly. As he patted the pocket of his suit coat he felt the reassuring rustle of the CN/CP flimsy there, and suppressed a smile. A few hours earlier he'd attended the daily nine-thirty caucus meeting at which the day's questions for Question Period were selected. They were always lively affairs, what with each of the delegation's members jostling and contending to have his or her question chosen to occupy that day's precious allotment of time to grill the premier and his cabinet over the issues that most affected the province. Although somewhat leery of the process—questions that had been vetted by the party and House leaders would be discreetly shared in advance with the relevant minister and his staff before the start of Question Period so that the minister in question could be briefed—Wardell had argued passionately on the importance of exposing the deplorable conditions in and around the Copper Cliff smelter. He had not, however, felt obliged to divulge the existence, much less the contents, of the telex from his Sudbury informant that he carried with him now.

Wardell had his quarry firmly in sight—Reginald McSorley-Winston, the Minister of Mines. Handsome, lantern-jawed and the possessor of a perennial tan even during the darkest days of another gloomy Ontario winter, McSorley-Winston was the son of a wealthy Bay Street banker. He was born and bred to rule, raised in the tony Toronto neighbourhood of Rosedale, educated at the very best schools—Upper Canada College, the elite private boys' school, the University of Toronto's most exclusive colleges—all just blocks away from these legislative precincts, all of this was the locus of power for Ontario's ruling elite. McSorley-Winston was a denizen of these waters in which Wardell, a rank outsider from the boonies of Northern Ontario, was just beginning to swim.

Ever the gentleman, and doubtless aware Wardell represented the largest mining municipality in the province, McSorley-Winston had greeted the newcomer from the north cordially enough, welcoming him warmly to the cozy old boys' club where power was exercised in the province of Ontario.

But, Wardell thought grimly, *he* was no gentleman, as McSorley-Winston was about to discover. Within minutes the benches and galleries were full, the Speaker had called the session to order, and Question Period had begun to unfold like the well-choreographed dance it was. Wardell impatiently awaited his turn.

At last the Speaker recognized the leader of Wardell's party who rose to ask his question of the premier. As usual the House was restive, with jeers and catcalls flowing freely on both sides of the aisle. It was a level of disrespect, bordering on hooliganism, that no elementary school classroom teacher would tolerate, but the Speaker, long accustomed to the lack of parliamentary decorum, only frowned. What did it matter, after all? No cameras or microphones were allowed in the chamber and Hansard, the official parliamentary record, would contain only the verbatim text of the questions, and the answers. The richly bound volumes, which would be passed down to posterity, would offer no hint of the infantile behaviour that accompanied the otherwise sombre conduct of the people's business.

The ever-smiling premier deftly side-stepped the question from "the leader of the third party," a slap in the face of Wardell's own party. As it generally did, the left-of-centre party had finished third in a three-horse race in the last election, an old wound the premier and his far more conservative cronies never tired of re-opening. The premier concluded his long-winded non-answer to the accompaniment of the usual rousing cheers and desk-thumping of his back benches and sat down, basking in the warm glow of approbation that rang from the gilt-encrusted ceiling of the Edwardian-era legislative chamber of Canada's most populous and richest province.

Now it was his turn to ask his maiden question in the House, and Harry Wardell nervously gulped a few swallows from a glass of water.

"The Chair recognizes the Honourable Member from Sudbury," the Speaker intoned, and Wardell, clearing his throat and buttoning his suit coat, rose to speak, his long frame unfolding rather like a snake uncoiling, about to strike.

"Thank you, Mr. Speaker. My question is for the Honourable Minister of Mines. Would he be good enough to tell us how the government polices the conditions in the metal smelters in this province and over which his Ministry has jurisdiction?"

McSorley-Winston, smiling grandly and breezily handsome as ever beneath his leonine mane of silver hair, rose in his place. He turned slightly to address the Speaker before turning to face Wardell. "Through you, Mr. Speaker. As the Honourable Member for Sudbury knows, our province is one of the leading mineral-producing jurisdictions in all of North America. . . as such, all mining, smelting, and refining activity in our province is overseen by inspectors from our Mines Safety Branch, which is charged with enforcing the provisions of the Ontario Mining Act, the statute regulating all mining activity in our province. . . I'm happy to say these inspectors are highly qualified professionals who do their utmost to ensure that Ontario's mines, mills and smelters are among the safest and most modern anywhere in the world." McSorley-Winston, well pleased with his answer, shot Wardell a broad smile. His white teeth, set off by his impeccable silver hair and deep tan were dazzling.

Wardell was on his feet almost immediately. "I'm sure we are all reassured, Mr. Speaker, to learn of the top drawer inspection services the Minister of Mines speaks so highly of. But I do have a supplementary regarding just that, Mr. Speaker. Can the Minister also assure us that his inspectors operate always in an arms-length manner regarding the companies they're charged with inspecting?"

McSorley-Winston sprang to his feet, but this time Wardell thought he detected a slight frown beneath the smug smile. "Why yes, Mr. Speaker our highly-trained and ever-professional inspection staff always operate with the best interests of our province's public in mind, as opposed to the owners and operators of Ontario's mines, mills and smelters."

As the Minister of Mines resumed his seat Wardell could feel a subtle sea change in the room. It might have been a rookie's imagination, but Wardell could have sworn there was a diminution in the hub-bub that perpetually filled the air of the grand old room. In the press gallery especially, the spectators, sensing that something was afoot, leaned forward eagerly to hear what was about to transpire.

Wardell was on his feet again, but this time the broad grin was on *his* face. "Always, Mr. Speaker? *Always?* Because I have it on good authority that as recently as yesterday the 'highly trained inspection staff' were at work in Inco's Copper Cliff smelter just outside Sudbury, conducting their diligent inspection *but only after calling in advance to alert the company that such an inspection was coming!*"

Here Wardell paused, partly to gather himself and partly for dramatic effect, and as he did so he bent his lanky frame low and forward over his desk. It was a visually arresting sight—a dangerous vituperative creature about to strike—and it was not lost on the press gallery. Now here was something novel, something *new*. The usual snide, cynical asides fell silent for once. Almost despite themselves, they were intent on what Wardell would say next.

The member for Sudbury suppressed a theatrical guffaw. "I only ask, Mr. Speaker, because I'm curious to learn whether the Minister of Mines is aware of the ah, shall we say close working relationship that currently exists between his minions in my riding and the International Nickel Company of Canada?"

A barely discernible blush began to colour the Minister's neck just above his shirt collar as he rose in the front benches to reply. "Well no, Mr. Speaker, I am not aware of any procedural irregularity in the inspection to which the newly arrived member for Sudbury refers . . . I can and do welcome the member to this House, but I feel I must caution him against making spurious, scandalous, and possibly even defamatory accusations against hardworking members of this province's civil service just for the sake of making headlines in tomorrow's papers!" The defiant Minister, jaw outthrust, shot his cuffs and, glowering at Wardell, sat down.

Wardell was back on his feet in an instant, but this time he had a small piece of paper in his hand. "Oh ho, Mr. Speaker, these are not empty allegations to which I refer." He waved the paper over his head. "I have here indisputable evidence that the International Nickel Company was indeed forewarned of an inspection by the Minister of Mines just this week!"

In the Press Gallery competitors from the big Toronto dailies glanced at one another, and first one and then another headed for the exit. Their colleagues from television and radio quickly followed suit, and soon enough the Gallery benches were emptied of onlookers.

Harry Wardell was as surprised as anyone at the reception that awaited him just off the floor of the legislative assembly. It was a full-on scrum, with a crush of print reporters, notebooks at the ready, foremost, surrounded by a ring of photographers and television cameramen, flashbulbs popping and klieg lights glaring.

Wardell was quite startled at the crush. The mob was all shouting at once, yelling questions at him, but Wardell quickly gauged the upshot: what proof had he of Ministry-Inco collusion, and could they see it? At six foot seven inches, Wardell easily stood above the throng, and now he drew out the telegram and held it aloft. "As you can see, this telex, which was sent to me by a reliable source in Sudbury, predicts that a Ministry inspection is about to take place. Note carefully the date and time. I can assure you just such an inspection occurred the following day. . . Now my question is *did this Minister, and by extension this Government, know this collusion was taking place?*"

Wardell was careful to hold on to the telegram, flashing it only briefly so that the press corps could see the date and time for themselves. They were silent for once as they scribbled the details in their notebooks while cameramen focused their lenses on the paper in Wardell's outstretched hand.

* * *

"Copper Cliff smelter?" Foley Gilpin was momentarily taken aback by the question from Mike O'Neill, his boss and the Ontario desk editor of the *Toronto Globe and Mail*. "Yeah, sure I've heard of it. Why do you ask?"

Gilpin was surprised at the question because normally the flow of information on his beat was a strictly north-to-south affair. Unless a story made the wires his bosses in the Toronto newsroom were usually in the dark about developments in the Nickel City—unless, that is, he, Foley Gilpin, told them about it, usually in the form of a story pitch. And that was the way Foley liked it—with a two-hundred-fifty-mile buffer from the prying eyes of his bosses.

"The Leg bureau guys were pitching a story on it in the budget this morning, is all. . ." O'Neill pronounced it "Ledge," and Gilpin understood this as newsman's shorthand for "Legislature." "Thought maybe you'd've heard about it. . ."

"Uh, no. What was the story?"

"Seems your new MPP from up there, Warden, Woodley? "

"Wardell."

"Yeah, that's him. Well anyway he accused the Ministry of Mines and their inspectors of being in cahoots with the Company—claims they're tipping the Company ahead of time whenever they're about to do an inspection. . ."

"Oh yeah? Did he have any proof?" Gilpin knew that Wardell, while passionate, was not above a little grandstanding when it came to making headlines—or winning votes.

"He did, as a matter of fact, according to our guys in the Leg. . . Just wondered what you mighta picked up on this?"

The question caught Gilpin off guard. He immediately thought of his friend and housemate Jake McCool, and the countless horror stories his exhausted and disheartened young friend had recounted after coming off shift.

"As a matter of fact, I know someone who works in there. He says it's pretty grim."

"Tell me he's not another one of your union crazies up there, Gilpin?" The words were uttered in a low growl and were more exclamation than question.

Gilpin knew to tread warily. He had long since learned of the *Globe's* anti-union bias—anyone in a leadership position anywhere in the union hierarchy was immediately suspected of a hidden agenda, while all professionals and captains of industry were assumed to be honourable and, above all, credible, men.

"Why no. Sure, he's in the union, like just about everyone who works at Inco, but no, he's not a union officer. Just a regular rank-and-file type of guy."

"Figure he can get you any dope on Wardell's accusations?"

"Dunno Mike. Let me do some checking."

And that was how they left it. To Foley Gilpin's own amazement he had just been assigned to investigate "conditions inside the Copper Cliff smelter."

Harry Wardell was only slightly less amazed at the fallout from his "maiden question" in the Ledge. All of the big Toronto dailies covered the story, which inspired the city's radio and television newsrooms to do the same. Suddenly an obscure backbench MPP was everywhere in the Toronto news media.

All this attention took Wardell by complete surprise. Back in his hometown he couldn't buy even a shirt-tail brief in the local papers about his activities and causes. Try as he might through news releases, news conferences, or photo-ops, he was resolutely shunned by the company-controlled news media. Because he was neither Tory nor Liberal, Wardell was beyond the pale—a parvenu who had won election by bizarre statistical anomaly. In one memorable encounter, he had watched as one of the city's foremost television news directors ripped his newly-delivered press release to shreds right in front of him, throwing it ceremoniously in the newsroom wastepaper basket.

But now, in the much larger and media-rich city of Toronto, he was, suddenly, the man of the hour. The company, through its spokesman in the Toronto headquarters office, fended off Wardell's allegations as best it could, officially stoutly denying any impropriety regarding Ministry inspections before going off the record to dismiss Wardell as a callow newcomer obviously given to grandstanding in a clumsy attempt to make waves and grab headlines at any cost. . .

. . .But at ground zero the fight wore on. . .

To the casual onlooker, they appeared just another random group of smelter workers eating their lunch together in the grubby confines of the furnace building lunchroom.

But, in fact, the dozen or so men seated around the table were anything but random, their lunchtime encounter anything but casual.

All had been invited by the big, bearded biker-looking type who sat near the middle of the table. Across from him were Jake McCool and his friend Randall McIvor from the furnaces, flanked by carefully selected representatives from the myriad of other workplaces in the sprawling smelter complex. Most were former Mine Millers who Robert "Haywire" d'Aguire knew—and trusted—from Mine Mill days.

The air was sombre as d'Aguire cleared his throat and silence descended over the gathering.

"We're still playing silly numbnuts over in the converters. Same old shit, different pile. Open Number Three when they need production, close 'er when they take a Drager reading. She's up and down like a whore's drawers." D'Aguire stifled a sardonic grunt.

His words only deepened the silence around the table. Jake surveyed the gloomy faces around him. "So they play games with the Dragers. . . . What if we were to start taking our own readings?" Jake thought back to his Mine Rescue days. "Underground everybody on Mine Rescue was trained to use Dragers. . ."

"Yeah, but even if we took our own readings we're still playing with a stacked deck," a sintering plant worker protested, "what with the Company having the Ministry in its back pocket, and all. . ."

"So, who cares?" riposted Jake, warming to his argument. "Why not just take our own readings, being careful to keep a record of the time and place of each reading and any changes in material conditions that could be checked against the company's own production logs, like whether this or that converter is shuttered?"

"Jesus, McCool, keep your voice down!" d'Aguire hissed, holding his hands up, palms opened up at Jake, who was momentarily thrown off his train of thought. "Oh. Sorry."

"Yeah, well, like I was sayin' if we took our own Drager measurements and kept our own written record maybe we'd at least have some kind of paper trail we could use later. . ."

"But would anybody but us ever care?" the sinter plant worker asked dubiously.

"Ya know, there just might be somebody who would," d'Aguire concluded. He said no more, but Jake could see the wheels were turning.

As soon as his shift was over d'Aguire climbed aboard his bike, a '65 Harley Davidson pan head chopper, replete with chrome ape hanger handlebars, a fatboy gas tank with a candy-apple red metal-flake paint job, upswept fishtail pipes, and a high chrome sissy bar. The extended front forks, which were also chromed, made the thing next to impossible to turn in a tight space, but the bike was Haywire's pride and joy, built for show, rather than practicality. There was no doubt the big Harley was his proudest possession, and soon enough Haywire had kicked the machine to life, the unmistakable roar of Harley thunder crashing off the red-brick walls of the smelter complex. As he revved the engine the soul-satisfying reverb that began between his legs and echoed off the walls so loudly that it eclipsed even the ubiquitous, ominous low growl of the Copper Cliff smelter caused a tight smile to form on the lips of the dour d'Aguire. As he eased off on the throttle the pop-pop-pop of back pressure in the fishtail exhaust pipes told him that, even running cold the engine was perfectly balanced and in tune.

The big biker muscled the machine around in a circle, and soon enough he was in the wind, booting it down Balsam Street through the peaceful village of Copper Cliff where the accelerating roar of twelve hundred cubic centimetres of full-throated Harley thunder scared the stray dogs in the neighbourhood, and startled the housewives out sweeping their porches, leaving them staring after him in gap-jawed wonder. Within minutes he would be running on the open road to Sudbury, a wind-whipped fury, bent on a secret, private vengeful mission.

Although the International Steelworkers Union had won the certification vote over the old Mine Mill by the narrowest of margins—a scant seven votes out of over ten thousand ballots cast—the Steelworkers' newly-formed Local 6500 had at first been a union without a hall, owing to a court decision that awarded the old Mine Mill Hall on Regent Street to Local 598 of the Canadian wing of the International Union of Mine, Mill and Smelter Workers.

D'Aguire booted the big bike into fourth gear, finally, when he had cleared the small town environs of Copper Cliff and pulled onto the higher speed highway that ran east between Copper Cliff creek to his right and the high black mass of the slag piles on his left.

Local 6500 had been forced to bounce around town, moving from one rented premises to the next, none of which was capacious enough to properly house an organization the size of the upstart local, which had been so recently carved out of the bones of Local 598. Besides the need of a meeting hall large enough to accommodate thousands of Inco workers at one time, there was also the requirement of sufficient office space to house a considerable clerical staff that served the elected Executive Board, which governed the union's day-to-day affairs.

D'Aguire was forced to downshift once again as he approached the western outskirts of the city. The big biker had made this commuter run so often he no longer really saw the Big Nickel, a many-times life-size reproduction of a Royal Canadian Mint nickel coin, erected high on a barren hilltop overlooking both Sudbury and Copper Cliff. The thing was a cheesy, tourist-trap gimmick in the eyes of many Sudburians, but it worked, both as a milestone on the segment of the Trans-Canada Highway that connected Sudbury to Copper Cliff, and as a tourist magnet for the hundreds who trudged up the hill to share a Kodak moment standing, smiling, beside the base of the monstrous coin.

After years of searching, the Steelworkers' real estate agents finally located just the place—a redbrick pile at the corner of Frood Road and College Streets. Erected initially by the Royal Canadian Legion, which had never been quite able to fully populate the place, the imposing structure at 92 Frood Road was soon sold to the Steelworkers Union, with the proviso that the Legion's first floor memorial to fallen comrades never be removed. It never was.

The three-storey former Legion Hall, which had a spacious first floor auditorium that was nearly as large as the meeting hall of the old Mine Mill building, also featured a rabbit warren of offices on the second and third floors. It was ideal for the big new union local, and, by the time d'Aguire had woven his impatient way through the shift-change traffic that congested Lorne Street to finally park his bike behind the building at 92 Frood Road, it felt as if the place had been a union hall forever. He could tell at a glance around the parking lot that the hall was already half deserted. Typical. Day shift had just ended, and most of the Local's elected officers had already left the building. Each of the four table officers—President, Vice, Secretary and Treasurer—had his own reserved parking spot in a space designated by a stencil painted on the back of the building. Finding all four slots empty, d'Aguire wheeled into the President' space. As a loyal Mine Miller, d'Aguire had no particular regard for any of Local 6500's table officers, who had led the insurgency against Mine Mill before running for office as a right-wing slate. To the victor go the spoils, and in a union local the size of 6500 the top four executive posts were rich prizes indeed—full-time desk job positions in the union hall, a world away from the nasty, noisy dangerous business of actually working for a living. The perks of office included a prime designated parking spot closest to the back door entrance to the union hall like the one d'Aguire had, with an outlaw's quiet satisfaction, just appropriated.

He entered the back door, which opened onto a landing. To his right was a short flight of stairs from which an updraft brought the reek of stale beer and cigarette smoke. The hall's subterranean taproom. But d'Aguire's business was elsewhere, and he forged straight ahead, up another short flight of stairs, into the grand space outside the hall's main auditorium. The spacious lobby was deserted at this hour, except for a solitary figure sweeping the floor. The footfalls of d'Aguire's heavy-duty biker boots echoed loudly off the fake terrazzo floor, and the custodian looked up from his duties to nod at d'Aguire, who nodded back.

The janitor, Bill "Shakey" Akerley, was a familiar figure around the hall. Also a part of the anti-Mine Mill insurgency, d'Aguire knew Akerley had won his current post, which was a considerable promotion from shovelling conveyor belt spills in the smelter, for his undying loyalty to the Steelworkers' cause. Clearly wet-brained—there were even rumours that the man was illiterate—d'Aguire knew that Akerley was much more than the buffoon he appeared. He was the eyes and ears for the Local leadership up on the second floor, and the international union staff reps who occupied the third. They might desert the building on the dot at the end of dayshift, but Akerley remained well into the night, a trusted witness to everyone—and everything—that came and went in the big building after dark. D'Aguire had no doubt that his appearance would be dutifully reported, and duly noted, up on the second floor in the morning.

The double wooden doors leading to the auditor- ium, still called the Vimy Room, *pace* Canadian Legion, were on d'Aguire's right as he strode across the foyer toward the one office that was still func- tioning in the Union Hall. As he knew it would be, the door was wide open, and d'Aguire stepped through.

It wasn't much of an office—a cramped, cluttered, airless single room, smelling faintly of BO and long ago cigarette smoke. Its single interesting feature was a large, battered wooden desk, behind which sat Paul Sampson, Local 6500's Chief Safety & Health Committee Officer. The single fluorescent ceiling light that illuminated the room cast a ghastly, blue-tinted light down on Samson, who appeared pale and haggard in the unforgiving glare of the cool blue fluorescence. D'Aguire knew that from this unassuming space Samson had almost singlehandedly built 6500's Safety and Health Committee into a parallel structure nearly as extensive as the big Local itself, with a Safety and Health rep in each mine and shop floor. The impressive organization-within-an-organization did not represent any kind of threat to the entrenched Steelworker hierarchy, however—Samson was a trusted Steel loyalist, as were most of his horde of Safety and Health advocates. But this skeletal organization did provide another means by which a lowly rank-and-filer on the job could become active in union affairs and begin a rise through the union ranks.

Beside the extensive Safety and Health network, the same modest space d'Aguire had just entered also headquartered Canada's first union Inquest Committee, a unique innovation necessitated by the terrible fatality rate within Inco's Sudbury mines and mills. It was the Inquest Committee's grim duty to liaise with the deceased worker's family, providing what comfort it could, and to represent the widow at the inquest which followed every mining death that occurred in the province of Ontario. The Safety and Health and Inquest Committees represented a dynamic response to workplace realities, and a pioneering sense of innovation that placed Local 6500 in the forefront of North American trade unionism. Still a Mine Miller at heart, even d'Aguire had to give the Steelworkers credit for that, however grudgingly. Sudbury reporters working the labour beat had long since learned that, in this beehive of a union hall, this beat-up room was where the action was, and, as d'Aguire entered the room it appeared that Samson was being interviewed by an older, balding reporter whom d'Aguire did not recognize.

Samson glanced up at the big biker who suddenly filled his door frame. "Why here he is now! Just the man you need to talk to!" Samson gestured back and forth to the reporter and the biker. "Bob d'Aguire, Foley Gilpin—Foley meet Bob d'Aguire, our head Safety & Health Commiteeman in the smelter, and also a damn fine shop steward in there. Bob, Foley's a freelance correspondent for *The Globe and Mail*, and he was just asking about conditions in the smelter. . ."

D'Aguire eyed Gilpin dubiously, giving his usual excellent impression of a man not being impressed. "Yeah? Why is that?"

Gilpin, who was seated on one of the few pieces of furniture in the hole-in-the-wall office, looked up at the big man from his perch on what had once been a back seat in someone's carry all. "My editor down in Toronto asked me to look into it, is all. Good friend of mine works there, and he comes home with some unbelievable horror stories about the place. . ."

D'Aguire nodded, heavy-lidded and menacing, "Oh yeah? And who might that be?"

"Young guy named Jake McCool."

"Sure, I know him. His stories are all true. . ."

"That's what I was just telling Foley," Samson interjected. "But now he's asking if there's any way he could sneak into the smelter to see for himself. . ."

D'Aguire heaved himself into the only vacant piece of furniture in the office, an ancient desk chair that faced Samson's desk. The biker gave a noisy, dubious sigh. The chair gave a squeaky protest beneath d'Aguire's weight, but it held. "Oooh, man, I dunno. That would mean a sure trespass beef if he was to get caught. . . Paul, you got a minute? There's somethin' I need to talk to you about. . ."

Gilpin took the cue, and stood up to excuse himself. "Well, uh, I'll let you two talk in private," he muttered as he swiftly left the little office which, in the presence of the burly biker had suddenly begun to feel quite claustrophobic. . .

D'Aguire paused long enough, looking over his shoulder, to be sure Gilpin was out of earshot before he turned to face Samson. "We had a plant-wide safety and health meeting today, and that young Jake McCool came up with a helluva idea I wanted to run past you. . ."

The Gilpin Commune

7

A Dinner at the Gilpin Commune

Gilpin left the Steel Hall through the same door d'Aguire had just come in. On the short drive across downtown to his house Gilpin tried not to let his hopes race too far ahead of reality, but he was excited, there was no doubt about it.

When he arrived home dinner was already on the table and being served. Gilpin barely glanced at his housemates as he took his place at the table. They were a motley crew, to say the least. The main thing they had in common was that, unlike Foley, they were all in their twenties. Jo Ann Winter and Jake McCool were familiar faces; the others less so. Pierre Dufour was a new breed, at least to Foley. A new arrival in Sudbury, Dufour was a recent participant in a student uprising at a high school not far from the Nickel Capital. In a year when university students from Mexico City to Paris were launching open, and often very violent, rebellion against all forms of authority, Dufour and his confreres had conducted a peculiarly Canadian revolt—they had peacefully, but with an utter determination that belied their tender years—occupied the school cafeteria to underscore their demands that courses be offered in their mother tongue—French. The entire affair had caught their district school board badly off guard, and it had also captured the imagination of Canadian news editors eager to find a domestic angle that reflected the angry global zeitgeist of the spring of 1968. The protest was assumed to be of a piece with the burgeoning movement to gain independence for the French-speaking province of Quebec where a growing radical movement to have Quebec secede from the rest of Canada was gaining traction. When he'd first met Dufour, Gilpin had assumed the outspoken young Francophone was part of the same movement. But to his surprise, Dufour had been deeply offended. "Oh, no,no, we are not Quebeckers, and we are not like them one bit," Dufour insisted. "We are Canadians who simply want to live our lives, communicate, in our own language. We are not separatists, s'tie!"

Gilpin's friendship with young Dufour had begun in a venue that was fertile ground for animated conversation, amorous flirtation and more than a few one night stands—the basement of the President Hotel. The bar, in a long, narrow, L-shaped room that featured live music nightly from a raised bandstand in the corner where the two dog legs of the room joined, was a swirl of colour, movement, and noisy action much in vogue with the downtown Sudbury crowd who, still in their twenties, could drink, smoke and carouse until closing time and still manage to drag themselves out of bed with no more lingering ill effects than a wicked hangover.

"So you're not Quebeckers, but you support Quebec separatism?" Gilpin had to yell directly into Dufour's ear to make himself heard over the rumour and roar of the noisy taproom.

But once again, Gilpin learned, his stereotyping of French Canadians was badly off the mark. Dufour and his counterparts outside Quebec were, if anything, actually *opposed* to Quebec withdrawing from the Canadian confederation. Such a move would cost them their strongest leverage, in the form of millions of Quebec votes, that appeared to have brought them to the verge of securing their own newly-won, hard fought language rights as French-speaking minorities outside Quebec.

Now more confused than ever, Gilpin shouted another question into the ear of the young Frenchman. "And your accent—is that what they call *joual?*" Foley just assumed that the unique French Canadian patois common in Quebec—a corruption of the French word "cheval"—horse—was the dialect spoken by all French-speaking Canadians. His own rusty high school French told him the vernacular form he heard around him in the streets of Sudbury—and here in the bar of the President Hotel—was far from the so-called Parisian French he thought he'd been taught in school.

Dufour responded with a frown, and then laughed. *"Quoi? Que tu dis? Joual? Oyons! Non, non!.* Our French is—how you say it?—it is not perfect, but it is the speech of this place, of Nouvel Ontario, and not that of Quebec... Here we build our own..." Dufour struggled to find the right word, "...our own expression, our own culture, I suppose."

Gilpin nodded at this, hoping that his outward reaction masked his inward skepticism that such a lofty goal could ever be realized. The conversation came to an abrupt end when Dufour suddenly glimpsed a group of friends entering the bar, and motioned them over to the table. As he had warned Foley that it might happen, the conversation switched suddenly to French, excluding the transplanted American newspaperman from the discussion, which swirled on around him in a rapid-fire, staccato delivery French that was heavily accented in a way he'd never heard before and that left him wholly uncomprehending. This sudden inability to use his strongest single social attribute—language—left Gilpin feeling intensely uncomfortable.

This jarring slight, Dufour had forewarned Gilpin, should not be taken personally, rude as it was. For generations, Dufour explained, when a group of French Canadians had gathered in the presence of a guy who only spoke English they had switched to English as a matter of courtesy. A measure of civility, yes, but also another step down the slippery slope of assimilation, and toward the extinction of the French language in North America. No more. Now it was time for the English to meet them halfway. It left Gilpin dangling, the unwitting adjunct of centuries of Canadian linguistic friction, but the newspaperman, who had grown up in the overwhelmingly unilingual environment of Chicago, hung in there, intrigued by the evident charisma and dynamism of the French language militants, to say nothing of the attractive young women in their midst. And so he remained at the table, suddenly dominated by a language he did not understand, struggling, with little success, to comprehend the animated conversation that now swirled around him.

Back at his own dinner table in the stately old, red-brick downtown house Gilpin and his youthful friends had transformed into a "commune" of sorts, Gilpin's gaze fell on another relative stranger at the table, a young man named Jerry McNally. Far from his favourite housemate, McNally's presence was the result of the general election campaign then underway across Canada. A professional organizer for the Liberal Party of Canada, McNally was there because of Gilpin's long-standing friendship with Spike Sworski, the former President of Mine Mill Local 598, who had, after his ouster as union president, become one of the city's leading Liberals. It might have appeared an improbable political metamorphosis to many—the militant leader of a left-leaning union local, joining the mainstream Liberal party rather than the more left-leaning, social-democratic CCF, but Gilpin understood Sworski's choice completely. To Spike the CCF was the handmaiden of the Steelworkers Union, the political front for the powerful American-based union that had swept him from power and destroyed the old Mine Mill. It was a split Sworski could neither forget nor forgive. Instead, he'd found a political home in the more centrist Liberal

Party, and, as the general election campaign of 1968 geared up, the national party had dispatched him a youthful organizer in the form of young McNally in the hope the duo could capture at least one of Sudbury's two federal seats, which had been deemed as winnable and in play by the party's national strategists. McNally needed a place to stay during the campaign, and Spike had asked Gilpin to find room for McNally at the co-op.

McNally struck Gilpin as smarmy and too smug by half, all button-down collars, chinos and penny loafers, the cleanest-cut youngster at the table, and, judging by the way he was eyeballing Jo Ann, something of a lady slider as well. Jo Ann, who was also a Liberal party activist, didn't appear to be actually flirting with the preppy-style young McNally, but they were both euphoric at the turn their campaign had taken the night before.

Their party had been led into the election campaign by their new leader, who had become interim Prime Minister, succeeding Lester Pearson, the moment he was elected Party leader just three months earlier, a young, charismatic and largely unknown newcomer named Pierre Elliott Trudeau. As luck would have it Election Day had been set for June 25, the day after Quebec's National Holiday, St. Jean Baptiste Day. A proud Quebecker himself, Trudeau had elected to wind up the long campaign—which had been dominated by his magnetic charm and mass appeal, a phenomenon labeled "Trudeaumania" by the media—by attending the annual St. Jean Baptiste parade in his hometown, Montreal. The celebration was traditionally part celebration of Quebec élan, part rite of spring, part Bacchanal, and often the commingled high spirits had a way of bubbling out of control and into full-blown street riots. That year, much of the *indépendantiste* fervour was directed at the youthful Trudeau, who was regarded as a traitor to the Quebec cause for his decision to lead a federalist, national Canadian party. The mood turned ugly as the crowd began to vent its anger at the Liberal leader, first in the form of jeers and catcalls, then in the form of stones and bottles thrown at his front row seat in the reviewing stand. Trudeau's aides and the other dignitaries seated around him did what any sensible person would do—ducked and ran for cover, which was precisely what the interim Prime Minister's security detail urged him to do. But Trudeau would have none of it. Instead, he merely sat forward in his seat as if to gain a better view of the vitriolic attack upon him, a cool, smugly arrogant smile playing across his lips. It was a Cheshire cat-like expression Canadians would come to know all too well in the coming decades, but on that night, in the full glare of the media spotlight, with the Montreal Riot Squad charging and their billy clubs flailing, the man's steely determination electrified the nation, and buoyed the spirits of frontline campaign workers like Jerry McNally and Jo Ann White, who, as Gilpin could see, were clearly ecstatic at the prospects for their party when the polls closed in a few short hours.

In a way, Gilpin hated to burst their bubble, but he had other fish to fry. Once the salad had been passed around and everyone had had the chance to settle in, the reporter looked at his friend Jake. "Met a friend of yours today."

"Oh yeah? Who?"

"Robert d'Aguire."

"Oh! Haywire? Where'd you meet him?"

Gilpin shrugged. "Union Hall. Safety and Health Committee room." Then he eyed Jake quizzically. "Haywire?"

Jake shrugged in return, and smiled broadly. "Yeah, sure. Haywire's how he's known at work. Name suits him pretty well there. . ."

"Really! Is he that big a shit disturber?"

Jake nodded. "On the job he is, especially when it comes to health and safety. Why do you ask?"

"Because I just asked him to smuggle me into the smelter."

A forkful of lettuce headed for Jake's mouth stopped abruptly in mid-air. "You asked *what?*"

"I need to see inside that smelter, Jake."

"But Foley, why? It's dirty as all hell, very noisy, and very dangerous, especially for someone who doesn't belong there. I've told you a million times what it's like inside that beast. Isn't that good enough?"

Foley also put down his fork, and paused for a long moment before responding. "No, Jake, no it's not. I have to see what it is I'm writing about, have to be able to see it for myself. Feel it and smell it and taste it for myself."

Jake glowered at him across the table. "So you don't believe what I'm telling you about conditions in there, is that it? You think maybe I'm making it all up or exaggerating somehow? What'd he say?"

"He who?" Gilpin was momentarily distracted by his hot-headed young friend's belligerent tone. "Oh, Haywire. Well, he didn't say no, only that it was risky, especially if I got caught by company security."

Jake nodded. "Yeah, there is that." Jake's tone softened, and clenched fists gave way to clear-cut concern for his friend's well-being. Tensions around the table, which had risen suddenly to the boiling point, now dissipated as quickly as they had appeared.

"I just don't want you to get in trouble, Foley. Or to get hurt in any way."

"Yeah, I know, kid, I know. And I do appreciate that." Foley bit off the "but" that was on the tip of his tongue, thought better of it, and abruptly changed the subject.

Jo Ann whirled around and came at him the moment their bedroom door was closed. "Jacob McCool, how could you?" she hissed. "Sometimes I can't believe what a bonehead you are! Foley only wants to help, can't you see that? Why won't you help him get into the smelter?"

"Aw, Jo, come on now," Jake, taken aback, began defensively. "He doesn't belong in there. He has no business being in that place. It's no place for a— " Jake struggled to find just the right word—"a scribbler!"

Jo Ann's eyes widened in disbelief. "A scribbler! That's what you think the man is? Jesus, Jake McCool you mental midget! I buy you books and buy you books and all you do is look at the pictures! Foley Gilpin is our friend. When you wanted out of your parents' he took you in, and then me, too. Where would we be right now if it weren't for Foley Gilpin?"

She snorted at Jake. "Besides which, this 'scribbler' just happens to have access to the most influential newspaper in all of Canada. You say you want to clean up that smelter, but there's ways to kill this cat besides drowning him in Crown Royal, Jake!"

"*What? Where did that come from?*" Jake realized he was grinning now, despite himself. God, she turned him on, even when she was angry. And she always could make him laugh, even in moments like these.

Sensing Jake's hesitation, Jo Ann rushed into the pause to finish her argument. "Jake, with you guys it's always about bull, bull. You always think you can have your way by just smashing through things, by just punching people out. Look at Rafferty's gang during the Raids, going around beating people up because they were on the other side! So tell me: how did that work out for ya?" She hurled the defiant question at him, standing before him, green eyes flashing with anger, her hands at her side, balled into fists.

Jake swallowed. Her words hurt. The defeat of the Mine Mill was still a raw wound for Jake, as it was for many in Sudbury.

"Well, well," he stammered, groping for a response, "Foley was there for that, he was on our side, and I didn't see *that* as making much of a difference . . ."

She didn't miss a beat. "Yeah, but this is different Jake. You're not gonna win this battle out there in Copper Cliff! Toronto is where it'll be won or lost, because that's where all the power is, and I don't mean just the power at Inco. Look, didn't you tell me once that the province was pressured way back in the days of the open-bed roasters into building the smelter in the first place?"

"Yeah, sure, but that was way back in the Thirties and I don't see—"

Jo Ann cut him off with a wave of her hand. "What? You don't think history can repeat itself? But don't you see? See where Foley might just have some power now, in this new thing?

They don't call it the *Toronto Globe and Mail* for nothing, ya know, Jakey boy."

He stared, hard, into the green eyes he knew so well. This time he saw no mischief there, no longer any flash of anger. He saw only triumph.

8

The Lunch Bucket

It was there, at Foley's place, the next night at supper: a plain Sudbury nickel workers' lunch bucket, clearly used, plastered with stickers. When it was new, it had been an object of both utility and simple elemental charm, a lunch pail, yes, but one invented and manufactured entirely in Sudbury, designed and built to withstand the rigours of the underground environment. Gilpin eyed the object quizzically, its brushed aluminum surface now scuffed from countless scrapes and nicks and now almost totally obscured by stickers related to union politics. A little thicker than a cigar box standing on edge but not much larger, a well-worn stainless steel handle rested on its bevelled top. Foley reached out for the handle—the invitation was too obviously irresistible—and hefted the lunch box. It was perfectly balanced. Empty, it was light as a feather in his hand. But the lack of heft, Foley knew, belied the sturdiness of the thing, which had a million uses. If Sudbury could be said to have its own icon, this lunch box was it. Besides protecting a man's chow from the damp and dust underground or the dust and gas on surface, the lunch bucket also served as an impromptu stool, easily supporting a man's weight as he waited on the street corner for his ride to work. Knots of Inco workers could be seen on any major street corner at shift change time in those days, perched atop their lunch pails, patiently awaiting the arrival of their car pool to take them to Copper Cliff or Levack or Creighton or out to Frood. Even the heaviest man could position his lunch bucket on the edge of the curb, resting his boots in the gutter, and sit down on his lunch pail, his knees drawn up nearly to his chin. There was no question what the lunch pail, light as it was, would bear his weight. The thing was indestructible, and guaranteed for life. With growing curiosity, Gilpin unsnapped the tight clasp that sealed the contents of the lunch box off from the random rigours of Sudbury's workaday world. He opened the hinged lid—clearly the lid, angled like a mansard roof, was designed to accommodate a thermos or bottle of water—and peered inside. Here the dull aluminum finish was still unblemished and smooth. The thing was empty and spotlessly clean. Gilpin noticed Jake grinning across the table at his close inspection of the lunch bucket.

"Smelterman's gotta have his lunch with him, right Foley? Get a good night's rest, my friend. Day shift starts at seven, we leave the house at six."

9

Busted

The newly risen sun cast long slanting shadows across downtown Sudbury as the two men left the house the next morning. The air was fresh with the promise of a new day, and there was already a hint of the heat that would come later in the day. And it *was* a new day: the country had a new Prime Minister—Pierre Trudeau's incumbent Liberals had easily defeated their Tory opponents, led by an MP whose family owned a well-known Maritime-based underwear manufacturing company. Like a wave breaking against a stout seawall, the hapless Tory leader would hurl himself against Trudeau again and again, finally becoming known in Canadian political history as "the greatest Prime Minister the country never had."

Jake and Foley sat on the corner on their respective lunch pails, wrapped in a thoughtful silence that masked their apprehensions about the day to come. The silence continued on their ride out to Copper Cliff.

Roughly a thousand workers were needed to keep the insatiable maw roaring around the clock, its great furnace fires banked, its rivers of molten metal flowing. Not all of those workers were ever on site at any one time, of course, but day shift change was definitely highest traffic time at the Number One Gate, with hundreds of workers streaming in and out past the guardhouse at the gate.

And so it was that a non-descript middle-aged figure toting his lunch pail, his spectacles concealed beneath mandatory safety glasses, his slight potbelly likewise hidden beneath the same work coveralls worn by hundreds of his fellow workers, walked unremarked past the uniformed security guards in the guardhouse.

Foley Gilpin, sweating heavily inside the unaccustomed warmth of both his street clothes and a set of Jake McCool's borrowed coveralls—thoughtfully left unlaundered just for the occasion, and several sizes too large—carefully followed the directions he'd been given to the Number Three Dry.

Once inside what he quickly recognized as little more than a cavernous locker room Gilpin was greeted by a knot of quietly intense men. D'Aguire he recognized, but the rest were all strangers. Jake completed a round of introductions. Left unsaid was the fact that Gilpin was present on sufferance—many of the safety and health reps were cool about the idea of Gilpin's presence in the first place—but they had been won over by Jake's unstinting vouching for the reporter. Each of the strangers peppered Foley with questions—more like observations, really—reciting what seemed to Gilpin to be more like anecdotal evidence about how truly awful his own individual workplace was, urging the newsman to visit the converter aisle, the furnaces, Matte Processing, no, wait! The sintering plant!

The apprehensive Gilpin, who had been offered, and had accepted, a seat on a long wooden bench, glanced around the big room. He was relieved to see that it had cleared of other workers, who had doubtless gone off to begin dayshift at their appointed stations. This sudden flood of information was all very well, but it was evidence—hard, solid, factual evidence—Gilpin needed. He knew his sceptical editors in Toronto would demand nothing less.

Perhaps sensing his perplexity, d'Aguire suddenly raised his hand, in a mute signal for silence. To Gilpin's surprise and immense gratitude, the manoeuvre worked, and a hush suddenly descended over the unruly little band. "Now see here, you jokers," d'Aguire rasped, "s'pose we let this man tell *us* what it is he needs to see. . ."

Gilpin struggled to answer the question. The truth was, he didn't know what he didn't know. "Well uh, I want to see the conditions inside the smelter on a typical working day, I suppose."

With that the reporter pulled out his notebook and began to scribble a few preliminary notes. His anxious onlookers, drawn in a tight circle around him, fell into a respectful silence at the gesture, peering down at him as if they were witnessing a momentous signal. Soon enough d'Aguire had taken the impromptu meeting in hand, and an itinerary for

Gilpin's informal—and illegal—smelter tour was formulated: the diminutive reporter would be passed from rep to rep, and department to department, in a prearranged sequence. Each rep would provide Gilpin the directions to the next shop floor as he needed them.

Ad hoc as it was, Gilpin's tour was unfolding pretty much as planned until somewhere between the converter aisle and Matte Processing he got turned around. It scarcely mattered; he was done. This place was all that Jake had told him, and more. Conditions in the converters beggared description, and that *was* a problem: how to describe what he'd found to the paper's ever-sceptical editors, much less its readers? As for concrete, objective measurements, Gilpin vaguely recalled his friend Jake saying that the union had begun taking its own measurements. Maybe he could publish those numbers, and compare them with scientifically-approved threshold values. . . Gilpin was fretting over all this when he was spotted by Neil Rumford. The security guard was ruminating contentedly over his second stick of Juicy Fruit of the morning when his eye was drawn to a stranger who seemed to be wandering a bit aimlessly.

Rumford squinted at the odd figure, whom he did not recognize. There was just something a little strange about him, something that didn't quite fit. No one would ever mistake Neil Rumford for Dick Tracy, that was for sure. A product of the Law and Security program at the local community college, Rumford had always dreamed of becoming a cop, but when both the provincial and municipal forces had rejected his applications Rumford settled for the far less prestigious post of security guard at Inco.

Gilpin spotted Rumford, too, and was unnerved at the sight of his hulking figure, his barrel chest and big belly seemingly held in place by the Sam Brown belt he wore over his starched, freshly-pressed uniform. In another time and place Gilpin would have dismissed him as a faintly ridiculous character escaped from a Gilbert and Sullivan operetta. But not here. The newspaperman could sense Rumford's scrutinizing gaze, and it made him nervous. He wheeled around, and began to walk briskly toward an as yet uncertain destination. As rapidly as he dared, Gilpin darted around the corner of a towering brick building, hoping to put some distance between himself and the security guard, but even as he did so Gilpin could hear the tell-tale crackle of a walkie-talkie.

Foley never did quite break into a run, but he double-timed it around first one corner, then another, before slowing his pace so he could begin to catch his breath. He was really sweating now, but at least it appeared that he'd eluded his pursuer, and now Gilpin was able to turn his mind to his original problem: his headlong flight away from the big security guard had taken him even deeper into the heart of the smelter complex; but where the heck was he? He resolved to ask directions from the first rank-and-file-seeming worker he came across. But he was in the yard, as opposed to inside the smelter buildings proper, and it was still mid-morning of day shift, and there was not a likely candidate to be seen.

Gilpin had sidled his way around yet another corner seeking an entrance back into the smelter buildings when he was confronted by a pair of grim-faced security guards. Within an instant he felt a hand on his shoulder. It squeezed in a not-altogether friendly manner and did not let go. The newspaperman could tell by the weight of the hand and the sound of heavy breathing behind him that his pursuer had now become his captor. Still, it was one of the security guards in front of him who did the talking. "Excuse us, sir, but what is your business here?" Gilpin, speechless and still a trifle winded, could only shrug. His face, still flushed from exertion, reddened further.

"Yes, I see. Would you kindly come with us?" The hand on his shoulder tightened its grip.

The little foursome made its way indoors and through a series of cavernous chambers remarkable to Gilpin only for the roar of massive, mysterious machinery, and the dystopian fog of sulphur gas in such strong concentrations it made his eyes water. Eventually they passed through several glass-windowed industrial doors and the noise and gas of production grew faint. They were now traversing a rabbit warren of offices, the two security guards leading the little procession with Gilpin in the middle, and Rumford, still gripping Foley's shoulder, bringing up the rear.

He was ushered into a small, nondescript office where the main feature was a burly figure, attired in a rumpled brown suit, sitting behind a gray metal desk. Clearly this new figure had been expecting Gilpin, which the newsman accounted to the walkie-talkies each of his captors now had holstered in their heavy leather belts. The suited figure had the impassive, world-weary air of a man who has seen everything once. His most impressive facial feature was a bristling brown moustache below dark brown eyes that scanned Gilpin with alert interest. He nodded at the three uniformed guards who stood at attention around Gilpin, and they quietly left the room. Then the man behind the desk, who Gilpin took for an ex-cop, turned his full attention on Foley. By way of introduction he handed a business card across the desk. It read "Michael O'Hanlon, Director, Plant Security, Smelting and Refining Section, Ontario Division, International Nickel Company of Canada Ltd." Finally he addressed Gilpin. "And you are. . .?"

Foley realized he was still hyperventilating slightly. The result of the recent chase, yes, but also, the newspaperman was coming to understand, due to the revelations of that morning; he was on to a major story here. He did his best to conceal his excitement, and he was more than a little curious whether Mr. Flatfoot fully grasped the significance of his presence. Gilpin cleared his throat. "I'm Foley Gilpin, a freelance reporter for the *Globe and Mail*. I'm here on assignment from my editor, Mike O'Neill."

O'Hanlon regarded Gilpin with studied nonchalance for a few beats before reaching for the telephone on his desk.

Mike O'Neill was still in the morning budget meeting with Frank Blaney when the call came in, in the form of a gentle but unmistakable tap on the conference room door. "Yes?" The voice was Blaney's, in here, as everywhere in the Globe's Front Street West editorial offices, master of all he surveyed. Irritation at the interruption was clearly audible in the voice of the Managing Editor.

A copy clerk, tethered to an unseen telephone by an impossibly long coiled extension cord, popped his head through the door and looked straight at O'Neill.

He cupped his hand over the mouthpiece of the telephone handset. "Do we have a stringer up in Sudbury named Foley Gilpin?"

"Yeah, he works for me," replied O'Neill.

"'Cause he's been caught trespassing on Inco property, and he says you sent him there. It's Inco security on the line."

"Yeah, it was my assignment," O'Neill affirmed once again. *But Jesus Christ! He wasn't supposed to get caught in there! Of all the times to have this blow up. . . and in front of Blaney yet!*

Blaney was notorious for his encyclopaedic knowledge of all things Canadian east of the Red River, his stratospheric IQ, his razor-sharp wit, and his explosive temper. But now he only regarded his Ontario Editor with a slightly arched eyebrow and with what seemed, outwardly at least, mild interest.

"The Inco smelter? Didn't see that slugged anywhere. . ."

O'Neill only shrugged. "Yeah, well, it's only a stand-up piece."

Blaney nodded, apparently mollified at the explanation that Gilpin's assignment was nothing more than a "stand-up, anytime story," a low-priority news feature that would stand up indefinitely and that might make the paper only on a slow news day.

Or so it seemed to O'Neill at the time.

Though he couldn't hear it, Foley Gilpin could sense that the Inco security chief's conversation with the *Globe* had confirmed his earlier explanation regarding his presence in the smelter. As he hung up, O'Hanlon turned his stolid attention to Gilpin.

"You know Mr.-ah, Mr. Gilpin these premises are private property and that you were here without the owner's knowledge or permission, which means that you are guilty, at the very least, of trespass."

Gilpin nodded meekly. Time to tug the forelock and get the hell out of there. He'd had enough experience with cops the world over to know better than to argue with them. Never, ever argue with a man carrying a gun. He couldn't see for sure that O'Hanlon was packing, but he struck Foley as a man well acquainted with what in the States was known as Legal Concealed Carry . . .

O'Hanlon droned on, ". . . if, as your editors have just attested, you believe you have any business inside our plants at any time you are always welcome to contact our Public Affairs Department to pre-arrange a press tour. . ."

The upshot, in O'Hanlon's tone and demeanour, was that Gilpin was a minor irritant, a nuisance bug. Nothing more. At worst a mere gadfly, to be shooed away, and, if the time ever came, to be crushed summarily underfoot.

"And so, today, Mr. Gilpin, even though I would be well within my rights to do so, I will not charge you with trespassing on Company property. But I must caution you that if you are ever again apprehended on our property without authorization, then you most certainly will be charged, is that clear?"

Gilpin, breathing more easily now, merely nodded again, and he was almost beginning to speak, to stammer out—what? his obsequious gratitude?—when he thought better of it, and closed his mouth abruptly. There was no need for further self-abasement. This interview was drawing to a close, and Gilpin, for one, was glad of it.

And so, it appeared, was the security man, who had seemed weary of the thing—and of Gilpin—before it had even started.

O'Hanlon's minions, summoned by some unseen force, reappeared to escort Gilpin off the property. They accompanied him as far as the Number One Gate, where he was turned over to the security guard, a beefy, semi-comatose individual whose heavy-lidded eyes suggested to Foley that his breach of security was the biggest thing to happen on his watch in months, if not years. And with that Foley Gilpin found himself wandering alone through the vast expanse of the smelter parking lot. It would be hours now before Jake would finish his shift, and Gilpin, preferring not to wait, wondered how he would get back to town. He set out on his own, to walk out to Balsam Street and, eventually, to the main highway where he hoped to thumb a ride. He was well on his way before he realized he was still carrying his lunch pail, swinging it rather jauntily through the warming air of mid-morning. Time to doff the coveralls, which he did hopping awkwardly on one foot, curb-side on Balsam Street. But the lunch pail, which he had set carefully on the curb while he changed, the newspaperman was careful to pick up. Gilpin would keep that lunch pail for years, as a memento of his industrial-strength industrial adventure, and of the long train of events—little expected at the time—that would flow from it.

Foley knew better than to start writing immediately, much as he wanted to. For all that he had seen and experienced, he still didn't quite have his story, and he knew it. The constraints of "objective journalism" ruled out any reference to his brush with Inco secur-ity—the *Globe's* absolute strictures forebade any sort of first-person reference in a news story. Nor could he baldly assert what he knew as fact; every detail about conditions inside the smelter would have to be attributed to someone else, preferably the most cred-ible source possible. And so, after a few anxious days of waiting for the stars to align, Gilpin found himself once again in the Safety and Health office on the first floor of the Steelworkers' Hall. Crammed into the cramped space—made all the more stuffy by their very presence—were Jake McCool, Haywire d'Aguire, Randall McIvor, and several other union safety and health activists.

Out of a sense of deference and because he needed to be able to take notes, the chair behind the desk that was still the central feature of the tiny room was reserved for Gilpin, while Haywire and Jake kicked back on the old truck seat. One by one in a breathless rush each of the union men took turns explaining his workplace within the smelter complex, describing in almost loving detail what the newsman had viewed during his recent "tour"—details that had been lost on Foley in the heat, confusion and paranoia of the moment. Gilpin, in turn, questioned each of them about his individual job description, rarely looking up from his notepad as he furiously scribbled note after note. Once he felt he'd mastered the big picture—the daunting nuances of one of the world's largest integrated metallurgical complexes—Foley began zeroing in on the heart of the matter: specific monitored emission levels within different parts of the plant, exactly where and when the measurements were taken, and by whom, and how those readings compared to maximum emission levels mandated by provincial law, or, where no such laws existed— which was more often—"suggested threshold values," weasel words that stank to Foley nearly as much as the crudely lettered files before him, on which he could still detect the faint reek of sulphur from the plants. He might be a stranger, but each of the union activists was gradually won over by the bespectacled little man at the desk, whose sincere interest in a subject so vital to each of them was abundantly clear. They took turns solemnly opening drawers in the battered filing cabinets that lined the walls of the little room, pulling out files, and laying them on the desktop beside Gilpin's notebook. Even though it was Saturday, and only Gilpin was being paid for his time, there was no place else on earth they would rather be, no issue closer to life and death.

After a few hours, Foley Gilpin found himself developing a severe case of writer's cramp, along with a sense of sheer exhaustion at the intensity of the session. Finally he drew a deep breath, flipped his notebook closed, and sat up straight to establish eye contact with the eager, earnest men who surrounded him. "Oh, and one other last thing," one of them insisted. "The company opens up the vents at night, when they figure nobody's watching. I bet the sulphur levels downtown go through the roof." The others around him nodded, as if to confirm that this practice was almost as well known and routine as it was illicit.

"Well fellas, okay, I think that's it for now," Foley concluded, eager now to wrap up the whirlwind session and to get home to begin organizing his hectic notes and impressions into the cool, dispassionate prose style that would pass muster with his editors at the *Globe and Mail*.

It took Gilpin about two days to order his notes and firsthand observations into acceptable *Globe* style. He had long ago concluded that interviewers and members of the public-at-large, though well meaning, widely misunderstood the writing process. They tended to get hung up on the physical *act* of writing (where? when? how many days a week? hours per day?) rather than the more abstract and less measurable and visible process that, perforce, had to precede the actual act of writing. Organizing the raw material into serviceable narrative shape, formulating a compelling lede (arguably the single most important part of the entire process) and, inevitably, what research material to leave out.

The resulting effort, though filed in early July, did not appear until September, after the Ontario Legislature had resumed sitting following its annual summer hiatus. Gilpin had all but given up hope of ever seeing his smelter story in print when he received a call from O'Neill in Toronto.

"Listen Foley, you remember that stand-up you did on the smelter up there?"

Gilpin tried to mask his surprise at the question, even though his heart skipped a beat. Maybe his story *wasn't* on the spike, after all. "Yeah, sure."

"Yeah, well, we'd like you to do a sidebar to kind of personalize the main: how does all this affect the life of the average smelter worker, just some typical guy. Got anybody you could build this around?"

Foley thought instantly of Jake. "Yeah, sure, Mike, I can do that. How many words and when you want it by?"

O'Neill paused to do a quick mental calculation. "How 'bout next Friday in time for the Saturday bulldog?"

As he'd more than half expected, Jake balked at the idea of becoming the subject of a newspaper story.

"But why me? I've only been in the smelter a short time. You should do Haywire, or one of the guys who've been fighting for years to clean up that smelter."

"Aw, c'mon, man. I already know you—hell, I know your family—your dad, and even your uncles. C'mon, Jake, cut me some slack, here. Most of my research for this is almost done. All's I need is fifteen minutes of your time—twenty minutes, tops."

The discussion took place at the dining room table the next night, Jo Ann sitting next to Jake following every word with close attention. If Foley knew her—and by now he knew both members of the young couple quite well after having lived with them both on and off for the better part of five years—Jo Ann would have something to say to Jake on the matter later, behind closed doors.

And indeed it was a seemingly chastened, even hang-dog Jake who approached Foley at the coffee maker the next morning.

"Look. I'm still not crazy about this, but how 'bout we get it over with, and sit down tomorrow night?"

Foley agreed with alacrity, and evening found the two of them sitting face to face at the dining room table, Jo Ann, at Jake's side, also facing Foley.

Gilpin drew Jake out about his experiences working in the smelter generally, his overall work history at Inco, and the fact he was a second generation Inco worker, before prompting him to recount the story of his rescue of the injured co-worker who'd attempted the fatal short cut on the smelter floor. (Gilpin figured he could use the news release the company had issued praising Jake after the incident to bolster Jake's credibility in his story.)

Vast smelter complex skirts, often flouts, provincial regulations, workers say

By FOLEY GILPIN
Special to the Globe and Mail

SUDBURY—The huge Copper Cliff nickel smelter located just four miles west of this city often violates Ontario atmospheric emission standards while government inspectors quietly turn a blind eye, veteran workers at Inco's Copper Cliff smelter charged here yesterday.

The Inco employees, all seasoned health and safety advocates and members of United Steelworkers Local 6500, which represents the company's 11,700-strong hourly-rated workforce, charge that inspectors responsible for enforcing provincial regulations governing air pollution both inside and outside the sprawling industrial complex often call ahead to warn company officials of impending inspections.

"It's a pattern we've seen again and again," said Richard d'Aguire, a veteran overhead crane operator in the converter building, where the air and dust pollution is often so intense that Mr. d'Aguire's crane, which moves huge ladles of molten metal from one end of the building to the other, cannot be seen from the floor of the building, an area known as the converter aisles.

Mr. d'Aguire contends that Ministry inspectors routinely collude with the smelter's management to cover up violations of workplace health and safety and environmental regulations, a charge the company denied in a news release issued yesterday. "As has always been our practice, we operate the Copper Cliff smelter in a safe and responsible manner that conforms with, and often exceeds, provincial air quality standards."

But the company's own safety statistics, which reveal there were more than 5,000 lost time accidents at its Sudbury operation in 1967 alone, lend credence to the allegations of the union health and safety activists. Particularly disturbing to many was a fatal accident that occurred in the smelter's furnace building last June.

see "Sudbury" page two

O'Neill was true to his word, and the piece ran page one of the Saturday edition, the paper's largest circulation day.

Besides earning Foley his first front page by-line, his sensational take-out on the smelter also triggered a spate of local Sudbury media follow-ups or "matchers" throughout the following week. Although normally loathe to feature any news coverage even remotely critical of the huge nickel company—which had long since become the city's leading advertiser—even Sudbury's news editors were hard pressed to ignore a breaking national news story in their own backyard.

Foley's *Globe* story also featured a generous sidebar profile on Jake McCool, wrapped around the photo that Gilpin had managed to persuade a reluctant Jake to pose for outside the smelter plant gate, the smelter stacks looming, belching ominous smoke, in the background.

Because Sudbury newsrooms normally shied away from any sort of substantive coverage of Inco, their reporters had neglected to cultivate any sources of their own on the labour beat, and so when the time finally came to cover the smelter situation they defaulted to the one easily identifiable source who was already known on the story—Jake McCool. His youth, telegenic good looks, and strong local roots made him a natural go-to source for Sudbury reporters scrambling to match Foley's scoop.

Jo Ann was absolutely stunned at the reaction to Foley's story in the week that followed. Wherever she went—the hairdresser's, grocers, even the public library—the same conversation repeated itself over and over: "Wasn't that your boyfriend I seen in the news?" "I thought so!" "Oooh, he's kinda cute! Better keep an eye on him, honey!"

She was struck by how often the kibitzers expressed support for what Jake was saying and doing about conditions in the smelter. But then, who among them hadn't complained about the thick, gaseous palls of sulphur smoke that often descended without warning over Durham and Elm, at the heart of the city's downtown shopping district?

At first Jo Ann ascribed this to the tenor of the times—her Jake, with his shaggy, boyish good looks and burgeoning moustache, was Sudbury's own answer to the hippie movement, with its emphasis on peace, love, and good vibes toward all living things, Mother Earth, above all—but as her friends' reactions continued to unfold, it gradually dawned on her that the issue was shifting subtly, that a kind of tipping point had been reached, unexpected and therefore unheralded: what had begun as a workplace movement had struck a raw nerve in the entire community. Wherever you went, after all, in the barbershops, hockey rinks, or beer parlours, everyone knew someone who knew someone who had a brother, father or uncle who had endured a shift inside the smelting complex. Sudbury was a close enough knit community that such word—spoken or unspoken—travelled fast, and that what was perceived as an affront to the basic human dignity of one family was, at the speed of light, understood as an insult to all.

10

A Luncheon At the Albany

Charles Atlas Kemper III emerged from his shiny black limo and took the worn granite steps of the Albany Club two at a time. He entered the heavy, ornately scrolled, double hung bronze doors into a world of rich brown leather, discreet, indirect lighting, and muted conversations that decided the fates of huge corporations and swarms of working men in only the most hushed of tones. He looked up the magnificent entrance staircase—each step limned with a gleaming brass nosing, burnished daily—and there, at the top of the stairs, he found his host, smiling warmly.

Reginald McSorley-Winston extended his hand to Kemper. "Chas! So good of you to come! It's been far too long! Welcome back to the Albany!" He was heartily pumping the newcomer's hand. "Come, come", he gestured toward yet another grand entrance several paces distant, at the back of the clubroom, empty at this hour save for a few silver-haired grandees puffing contentedly on their cigars and quaffing brandy as they perused the morning's *Globe*.

The two men, attired in dark suits and black shoes shined to the brightest reflective sheen, strode toward the innermost sanctum, where they were greeted by a waiter in a starched and spotless white coat. He bent low at their approach and murmured "Mr. Minister" to McSorley-Winston and simply "Sir" to McSorley-Winston's guest, whom he did not know, as he reached out to open yet another set of double doors. The pair were then ushered in to the heart of the Albany Club, an imposing, high-ceilinged room lit principally by the natural light that streamed down through the stained glass skylights that formed the ceiling two storeys overhead.

As they took their seats McSorley-Winston was at last able to scrutinize his guest, who clearly was not from around here. He wore his snow-white hair just a tad longer than the usual Bay Streeter, and there was in his speech yet a tincture of the American Deep South, which had been his boyhood home. As the senior vice president of Inco's Ontario operations Kemper was an important enough player that the Natural Resources Minister had had his staff investigate Kemper's background and brief him prior to their lunch. Born and raised in Kentucky's Blue Grass Country, Kemper had attended Vanderbilt University in Nashville, where he'd excelled as an undergraduate. He moved on to Duke Law School, where he graduated at the top of his class, a finish that merited the close attention of recruiters from the top New York City law firms. Kemper had landed a position with the *ne plus ultra* of the Wall Street firms, Sullivan & Cromwell. There he had rubbed shoulders briefly—

for he was a much younger man—with the likes of the Dulles brothers, John Foster and Allan. Senior partners who had parlayed their day jobs representing America's most powerful corporations into positions of great personal wealth and power, the Dulles brothers discreetly advised Kemper to buy shares, as they had, in the nickel company that was at the heart of the American military-industrial complex, but whose primary asset lay outside the States, in Sudbury, Ontario, and squarely within the purview of McSorley-Winston's Ministry.

To the Ontario politician the American tycoon's barely discernible accent, with its softened vowels, lent his voice a certain languid, almost purring quality which, to McSorley-Winston's ear, was not unpleasant, not unpleasant at all.

McSorley-Winston cleared his voice, and came right to the point. "So, Chas, I was hoping we might discuss the situation with your smelter up there in Sudbury."

Kemper frowned slightly before breaking into a warm smile. "And what 'situation' would that be?"

"Well, you know, the recent newspaper reports of rather, ah- deplorable working conditions and that sort of thing."

Kemper responded with a dismissive wave of his hand. "Oh come now, Reg, surely we can't allow ourselves to become too exercised by the sensationalized whining of a handful of union militants! You know yourself how the papers like to blow these kinds of matters up out of all proportion."

McSorley-Winston hesitated. "Ye-es, undoubtedly true. But the problem here, you see, is the Old Man reads those very papers every morning, and our mandate is nearing its end."

Both men knew the Minister was referring to the Premier of the province, a wily veteran of Ontario's ever-changing political landscape. An affably benign figure in public, behind closed doors he ruled his Tory caucus, and its Cabinet, with an iron fist, as McSorley-Winston knew all too well.

"Ah yes, I understand. But we had rather hoped that our contributions to the party's war chest might provide a certain, a certain *je ne sais quoi*, don't you see. . ."

"Yes," the government man nodded agreeably "you have certainly been more than generous, but times change, you see, Chas, and it seems there's some new—and very strong—feelings running through the public now concerning pollution and the dumping of toxic chemicals into the environment. Then there's this new book written by that woman down there in your country. . ."

"Oh come now, Reg!" the Inco man expostulated good-naturedly. "Don't tell me you're going to let a few kooky beatniks and do-gooder intellectual eggheads determine public policy here in your beautiful province of Ontario!"

"Well, I"—Kemper cut him off to voice an afterthought prefaced by a slice of his hand through the air. "To say nothing of a small rump of union ingrates, including one disgruntled soon-to-be-former employee. . ."

"*Soon to be?* You mean—" McSorley-Winston arched an eyebrow.

Kemper nodded. "The ringleader of this little cabal. He belongs to one of these outlaw motorcycle gangs, I'm told. Criminal record longer than the Albany's wine list, Reg." Kemper chuckled with the air of a man who hadn't a care in the world.

"I see," nodded McSorley-Winston. "And you hired this paragon of virtue exactly why, precisely?"

Kemper shrugged. "We required his skills at the time. But now I'm told there's been—or there's about to be—a flagrant act of insubordination, so. . ." Kemper punctuated his sentence with another slashing gesture of his hand through the air, only this time it was across his own throat.

The conversation was interrupted twice—first by the waiter who took their lunch orders, then by the sommelier who turned to McSorley-Winston to order the accompanying wine from the Albany's justly celebrated wine cellars.

After a moment's deliberation the Ontario Minister selected a medium-bodied dry red, something that would pair perfectly with the food order, which was for the Albany's legendary noon-hour *spécialité de la maison*, the succulent baron of Angus beef, served *au jus*, Yorkshire pudding and horseradish. Both men ordered their roast beef medium rare, as they both liked to see a little blood on their plate.

Car telephones were expensive and cumbersome things in the 1960s, but Chas Kemper, like all of the top Inco brass, had one in his limo which he reached for even as the big car pulled away from the front of the Albany.

With the push of a button he was instantly connected to the company's senior man in Copper Cliff. The carefree mien he had displayed so convincingly in the club just now was gone.

James Rutherford, President of Inco's Ontario Division, groaned inwardly when the button on his desk telephone reserved exclusively for incoming calls from corporate headquarters began to flash—such calls were never good news, but he picked up. "Yes?"

The silky southern voice which had, just moments before, seemed so pleasant to the Ontario Minister of Natural Resources, had now turned to cold steel. The whip of the lash.

"Good afternoon, James," Kemper began pleasantly enough. "I do believe we have a bit of a problem down here, and I goddamned well want to know what you-all're gonna do about it!"

James Rutherford felt the lasagna he'd just enjoyed at lunch over at the Italian Club curdle in the pit of his stomach as he listened in silence to Kemper's recitation of his own lunch with McSorley-Winston.

"Yes, Chas, I understand. It'll be taken care of, I promise you that." Butter wouldn't melt in his mouth, but Rutherford hated being chewed out by his superiors as if he were some low echelon junior supervisor fresh out of engineering school.

Without daring to seem impolite, Rutherford wrapped up the call as quickly as he could. He seethed as he hung up the phone. Here he was, President of Ontario Division, the entire Sudbury operation that was the very fundament of Inco's pre-eminence in the global mineral trade—to say nothing of the most powerful military machine the world had ever seen—being dressed down like a sweeper on the shop floor. Still, he knew he had a problem, but he also knew just the man to help him fix it. He buzzed his secretary. "Get me Mike O'Hanlon in Plant Security. I want to see him right away."

It happened without warning, at the end of an otherwise forgettable shift. Jake, along with Haywire and Randy McIvor, was just changing into his street clothes when the goons charged into the dry.

There were three of them—Inco security guards in full uniform—and they went after Haywire first, body slamming him into the lockers with a terrific metallic crashing sound as dozens of steel locker doors rattled in their frames.

"Hey! What the fuck!?" Haywire, still naked from the waist up, instinctively clenched his fists as he struggled to regain his balance, his back against the lockers. As soon as he could, Haywire threw a punch—a haymaker right that struck only air—and his attackers, who surrounded him now in a tight circle, stepped back in unison.

"Yeah, that's right, tough guy," one of them sneered. "Ya want some of this? C'mon then! Ooooh, big tough scary biker! Guess you're not so big and scary here though, eh?"

Jake, though as startled as the rest of them, narrowed his eyes at the taunts. They were baiting Haywire, who was even then gathering himself for an all out counterattack. "No! Wait!" Jake yelled suddenly, jumping in between Haywire and the security guards. "It's a trap, a set-up! Don't do it, Haywire! They *want* you to poke them, don't you see?"

But Jake was too late. Haywire had already rabbit punched the loudmouthed security guard, belting him right in the lip.

The beefy guard's head snapped back, and he back-pedalled, but he maintained his balance, though he was startled at the swiftness of the blow. Instinctively he put his hand to his lip. It came away bloody.

"That's it, d'Aguire, you asshole!" he screamed, enraged at the sight of his own blood. "You're done! That's assault with intent! You all seen it! This man assaulted me! That's a Step Five, for sure! Stand aside from that locker!"

D'Aguire, with a quizzical look at Jake, did as he was told. The wide-bodied guard practically tore the door off Haywire's locker. Its contents came out flying in a flurry of overalls, workboots, plastic shopping bags. "Here it is! I got it!" the big man crowed, and he emerged from the locker triumphantly holding—a Drager!

After flipping the device to one of his partners the big man rounded once again on Haywire. "Guess you ain't such a big man right now, huh d'Aguire?"

Even with his back turned Jake could feel Haywire tensing, about to launch another blow. Jake sidled back and forth to thwart Haywire. He was face to face now with the bully boy guard himself, and it was all he could do to suppress the overwhelming urge to lash out at Haywire's tormenter himself. But he knew better. Ever since his mine accident his scrapping days were over. Even if he escaped serious injury in the fight, Jake knew Jo Ann would kill him when he got home.

The other rent-a-cops tossed Jake and Randall's lockers, seized their Dragers and retreated from the dry, but not before Haywire and the lippy guard had exchanged a few choice words.

"You know you're finished d'Aguire! The minute you hit me that was instant Step Five. You're gonna have plenty a' time to polish up that fancy bike of yours."

Haywire by now was sitting on the wooden bench in front of his locker, distractedly flexing his right arm, the fist of which had just clipped the beefy security guard. "Ah, Rumford, you're such a fuckin' goof. Why don't you fuck right off?"

"There!" the security guard was practically bouncing up and down suddenly, pointing at Haywire. "See that? He was touching his club crest at the same time he was calling me names! He's threatening me, uttering threats! You all saw it!"

It was true Haywire had a reproduction of the Wheelers club patch tattooed on his right bicep, but the gesture had, in Jake's eyes, been totally absent-minded and innocent.

The security guards, finally, began to back out of the dry, each of them clutching a Drager.

But before their shift was over Jake, Haywire and McIvor came to understand that the attack in their dry was part of a much larger plan. Locker searches had become standard throughout the smelter complex, and lunch boxes were also searched as men left the property.

In the short term, at least the Company's pushback was successful, with hundreds of Drager meters seized.

The union's initiative to monitor workplace conditions inside the smelter was now crippled. Even worse, their leader was finished. "Haywire" d'Aguire was, as Charles Kemper had predicted, fired from his job for striking, and threatening, a Company security guard on Company property.

The union moved to grieve the dismissal immediately, but the damage was done. It could take years for Haywire's grievance to wend its way through the preliminary stages of the grievance process before finally winding up in arbitration. In the meantime there was no way around it: they had lost their leader.

11

Constituency Work

Like most Ontario MPPs, Harry Wardell took advantage of any adjournment in the legislature to return to his home riding to catch up on constituency work—tasks, many of them mundane, but still quite necessary—that could not be fully accomplished from Toronto.

On this occasion he was pleasantly surprised to find reporters from the local Sudbury news media anxious, almost eager, to speak with him. This was a marked departure from the norm, when he often felt he could wander around the downtown intersection of Durham and Elm Streets buck naked and still not draw flies when it came to local news coverage.

Wardell reckoned, rightly, this was owing to the fact he'd been quoted in Foley Gilpin's groundbreaking exposé on the Copper Cliff smelter.

On this day, however, he was taking time out from his busy rounds of the city's newsrooms to visit his old pal Paul Samson at his little hole-in-the-wall office on the first floor of the Steel Hall.

To Wardell's surprise, he found the union man quite upbeat.

Like every other insider in the closely-knit Sudbury NDP/Steelworkers' activist community, Wardell knew all about the reverses Samson's smelter clean-up crusade had suffered with the firing of d'Aguire and the seizure of the union's Drager measuring tools.

"It's a great day, Harry," Samson insisted as he shook Wardell's hand.

The legislator, fresh in from Toronto, had his doubts. "Oh yeah? How so?"

"Just got off the phone with Pittsburgh, and they've authorized me to buy as many new Dragers as we need," Samson beamed.

Wardell *was* impressed, and he paused to ponder the full significance of Samson's news. Clearly, the United Steelworkers' International Headquarters in Pittsburgh was still keenly following developments in the big Sudbury Local it had struggled so long and hard to wrest away from the old Mine, Mill and Smelter Workers organization. Like most Sudburians, Wardell well remembered the days of bitter, often bloody, inter-union struggle between Steel and the old Mine Mill. He'd no idea what a Drager meter cost, but the fact that Pittsburgh had just given Samson what was effectively a blank cheque was sensational news indeed. So much for the old Mine Mill allegations that Sudbury's dues dollars would all flow south to Yankee-land, never to be seen again! And Wardell had to wonder, in passing, if a much smaller organization like the Mine Mill could have afforded the kind of financial backing Samson had just received from the much larger Steelworkers Union.

The news that greeted Wardell that morning lent credence to the rumour he'd heard in Toronto Steelworker circles that the big Inco local had been designated for an outsized role in Steel's strategic scheme for the entire Canadian economy; that it was being groomed to break ground for thousands of other industrial workers in Ontario's heavy industry, the heartland of Canada's economy. With its sheer heft in numbers and battle-tested troops, Sudbury's hard rock miners and smelter workers were a natural choice to break through at the bargaining table, and so "the Inco pattern" was on the verge of being born—what the Steelworkers' "shock troops" won first at Inco would set the target for union members at Canada's largest steel manufacturers in places like Hamilton, Ontario and Sault Ste. Marie. All these thoughts and premonitions flashed like sudden shivers through Wardell's mind as he stepped forward to once again shake hands with Samson to congratulate him on his latest—and most welcome—news.

"Hey, Paul! That's great! Any news from the Company?"

The smile was suddenly wiped from Samson's face. "No, shit. They're cutting us no slack on d'Aguire, won't return my phone calls. But they did send me a letter."

"Oh yeah? What'd it say?"

Samson grimaced. "Oh, nothing much. The usual PR bullshit. Made me wonder if anyone over there even bothered to read *my* letter."

"Sorry to hear that, Paul. What a buncha bastards." With a sigh Wardell threw his lanky frame down into the guest chair that faced Samson's desk. "Any ideas what we do next?"

"Well, this dealing with the Company is getting us nowhere . . . any chance of a meeting with the Ministry?"

Wardell grunted. "That sonofabitch McSorley-Winston is so far up the Company's arse that only the soles of his shoes are showing. You know that, Paul. Not sure what good a meeting would do at this point."

But after a brief, gloomy silence Wardell glanced over at the union man. "But if you think it might help, sure I can try for a sit-down—did you copy the Ministry on your letter to Inco?"

Samson nodded in affirmation.

Wardell called McSorley-Winston shortly after his return to Toronto. As usual he reached only the Minister's bored-sounding battle axe of a secretary, who made little effort to disguise her personal disdain for Harry. She took Harry's message and promised that the Minister would return the Sudbury MPP's call at McSorley-Winston's earliest convenience.

Wardell thanked her and hung up, expecting a wait of indefinite, though likely quite prolonged, duration, but to his surprise the Minister called back the same afternoon.

"Harry!" Wardell was taken aback at the cordiality of McSorley-Winston's greeting. He hadn't realized they were on a first-name basis, but what the hell?

"Hello, Reg, thanks for returning my call. Listen, I wonder if you'd be good enough to take the time to meet with one of my constituents to discuss the situation up at the Copper Cliff smelter?"

"And this constituent of yours—does he have a name?"

"Yes, oh sorry, yes. Of course. Paul Samson. He's with the Steelworkers Union."

"Name's familiar. Just happened to see it on a letter that crossed my desk only last week."

This admission surprised Wardell. Maybe they *were* getting on the radar, after all. But Harry couldn't shake the feeling that he'd missed something somewhere. McSorley-Winston's sudden bonhomie, his familiarity with the file, the fact he'd returned Harry's call in the first place, all of this just didn't quite add up.

Still, he wasn't about to look this gift horse... "How about next week?" he pressed.

There was a momentary pause as McSorley-Winston pondered. "Ye-es, I'd like to get my senior staff in on this, but yes, I think next week could work for us."

"Excellent! I'll let Paul know right away so he can make travel arrangements."

The date, time and venue were quickly arranged, and the call ended as cordially as it began, leaving the MPP for Sudbury as bewildered as ever about his apparent change in status, and about the sudden elevation in profile of the entire matter.

12

A Chance Encounter

Just as they took turns cooking dinner every night, so, too members of the Gilpin co-op alternated the weekly chore of grocery shopping, and today was Jake's turn.

He had just turned into the cereal aisle when Jake thought he spotted a familiar figure at the far end of the store, but his back was turned, so he wasn't sure. Intrigued, Jake quickened his pace, perfunctorily grabbing items off the shelf and throwing them into his buggy—Harvest Crunch cereal for Foley, rolled oats for porridge for practically everyone else—in an effort to catch up to his quarry.

Jake hurriedly turned up the next aisle, and found himself within earshot of the elusive figure he'd spotted earlier—or so he thought.

"Bob?" he ventured in a voice pitched low enough not to draw the attention of perfect strangers. But it was no use. The white-haired figure in front of him simply continued his own shopping in his comfortable, unhurried pace.

"*Bob! Hey Bob!* Jake repeated, louder now.

Eventually, finally the older man stopped, turned, and broke into a broad smile.

"*Jake! Is that you?*" Bob Jesperson extended his hand and began pumping Jake's own with evident, unabashed pleasure. "How are you feeling? Did you ever come back to work, finally?"

Jake nodded, and began looking his old work partner up and down. Bob's lively blue eyes were unchanged, but something about his glasses had. A horizontal line now crossed the lenses, partially obscuring Bob's beaming blue eyes. Bifocals, Jake realized.

"Yeah, yeah, I'm fine, but the doc wouldn't let me go back underground, so I'm at the smelter now. Been there for a while now. But what about you? Still at Frood?"

At first Bob, who now seemed frailer than Jake remembered him, and slightly stooped, leaned in toward Jake. "Eh?"

Jake swallowed, felt dismayed, and was beginning to repeat his question when Bob, at last, responded.

"Naw, they force adjusted me out to Levack."

"*Levack?*" Jake was stunned by the news. The mine at Levack was a good forty-five minute drive from Sudbury on a notoriously treacherous highway. "Levack! Wow! Helluva drive out there, huh?

"Eh?" Again the man who'd taught Jake the art and science of mining seemed to have trouble hearing him.

"Oh. Yeah the drive's a bugger, for sure."

"Especially in winter."

"Especially in the winter for sure," Bob affirmed solemnly.

"What's it like down there now, Bob? You know, working underground?"

Jake's former mentor smiled ruefully at the question. "Ever'thing's changed, Jake. You'd hardly recognize the place. There's way fewer men than there used to be. . ." Bob shook his head, deep in thought.

". . .It's the new machinery we got now. . .You wouldn't believe these new jumbos, and there's scoops don't even need drivers! Trammers stand off to one side and run 'em by remote control, just by pushing around this one button attached to a controller box attached to their belt, somethin' they call a 'joy stick'! Damndest thing!"

Jake had heard of such things, which were much ballyhooed by the Company, whose Public Affairs Department loved to tout all the latest technological advances in its operations. These wondrous new devices were so photogenic! That they often also led to the elimination of jobs wholesale while at the same time boosting both productivity and profitability was a factoid there was no great need to mention, but behind closed doors in Copper Cliff and the Albany Club this was bruited, and all those in the know agreed that the overall calculus computed perfectly.

13

Lock, Stock and Barrel

Just as they had agreed, both Harry Wardell and Reginald McSorley-Winston worked hard to hastily convene a meeting of key players—except the Company—concerned with conditions at the Copper Cliff smelter.

The meeting was held at a splendidly appointed board room in an historic limestone tower facing the Legislative Assembly known as the Whitney Block. All McSorley-Winston's Deputy Ministers were there, along with many of their Assistant Deputy Ministers, also known as ADMs. Facing this solemn, highly paid assemblage across the imposing hardwood table that had been burnished and polished to a warm, nearly reflective sheen were the two lone Sudbury reps, the gangly Wardell and the rumpled Samson, who looked as if he had just emerged from a cramped, turbulent flight from Sudbury, which he had.

Once they were all seated McSorley-Winston called the meeting to order, and after a brief round of introductions, he re-stated the purpose of the meeting.

"Paul and Harry, I wanted to kick off this thing by sharing with you a letter that contains a written statement of our latest and best thoughts on the matter at hand."

With that, the Minister slid each of them an official-looking document, printed on Ministry stationary, that had been typed out in dense, single-spaced text blocks. The verbiage was so lengthy that it couldn't fit onto a single page. A second page was attached.

Wardell glanced at his copy with studied indifference, in an effort not to appear impolite to McSorley-Winston and his minions. He flipped over the top page out of idle curiosity to see who had signed such a weighty missive and found McSorley-Winston's signature, penned with its usual flourish.

Samson, on the other hand, picked up the document and began reading with intense interest.

Soon after Harry felt a tapping on the top of his right foot. It was Samson, signalling him surreptitiously under the table. Harry cast a subtle sidelong glance at his friend. With a barely discernible motion with his head, the Steelworker nodded at the door—signalling he wanted to meet with Wardell in private.

Harry cleared his throat. "Will you gentlemen excuse us for a moment?"

While clearly nonplussed at this unexpected delay in his meeting, McSorley-Winston had no choice but to comply. He smiled icily at Harry. "Certainly."

Samson grabbed his briefcase and the Ministry statement letter off the table and the duo made a hasty exit. Once they were clear of McSorley-Winston and his clique, Samson excitedly fished a paper from his briefcase and laid it on a table next to the Ministry's newly-released statement.

"I knew it, I just knew it!" Samson exclaimed. "I'm seeing it, Harry, but I'm not believing it! Here! Look here! And here and here!"

The union man was pointing to several paragraphs mid-way down the Ministry's document.

"Do you remember me telling you I wrote the Company a letter weeks ago, and all I got was a vanilla letter in reply?"

Wardell nodded. "Sure I do, Paul, but what's this all about?"

"Just look, Harry! Compare these two, tell me what you see! *I knew I'd read this before!*" Samson was pointing at the Ministry document, so bland it had bored Harry to tears. But now he bent over the letter on Inco letterhead, squinting at it for the very first time.

It was addressed to Paul Samson, United Steelworkers of America, (and was copied, Wardell noted, to the Ministry's District Engineer in Sudbury), and it purported to address "union complaints regarding gas and dust conditions in the Roaster Building of our Copper Cliff smelter. . ."

"Due to the nature of roasting and smelting operations and despite thorough and continuing maintenance procedures, conditions involving high SO_2 readings do occur from time to time in areas of the Roaster building. As the process is continuous. . . it is necessary to keep equipment operating despite these conditions. . ."

Wardell switched his attention to the Ministry's letter, where *he found the very same words*. The conclusions were also identical: "It would appear therefore that the conditions are highly exaggerated [by the union's health and safety monitors] and that the complaints are not justified." Suddenly the light came on, and Harry's jaw dropped. "You mean?. . ."

Samson, who was bouncing up and down with excitement, nodded. "Word for fucking word, Harry!"

Harry shook his head in disbelief. "You mean they didn't even change the punctuation?"

"Nope! The Ministry didn't even bother to re-write the Company's reply to me! I guess the District Engineer bumped it up here to the Park, and the Ministry just copied it over."

"What should we do now, Harry?"

Wardell's mind was racing at Samson's revelation, still trying to fathom its full ramifications.

"Just leave this to me, Paul. I'll take care of it. Let's go back in. Just leave these right here," Harry pointed to the incriminating documents on the table.

"Sure, Harry." And with that the Steelworker activist led the way back into the boardroom.

Samson returned to his seat, but Harry did not. Instead he paused directly behind McSorley-Winston, who was sitting with his back to the door they'd just entered.

Wardell placed his hand gently on the Minister's shoulder. "Reg, could I speak with you for a moment in private, please?"

Startled, McSorley-Winston turned around awkwardly in his seat in an attempt to see Harry, who towered over him. "*What?* Oh. Sure, Harry."

The two men left the boardroom and were immediately standing over the documents which Samson and Wardell had scrutinized just moments before. Wardell spoke first.

"Since you signed it, Reg, I'm assuming that you read the contents of the Ministry's official position regarding conditions inside the Copper Cliff smelter."

The Minister shot the Sudbury MPP a sharp "why-are-you-restating-the-obvious-I'm-a-busy-man" glance before shrugging. "Sure."

"Well then I'd ask you to look over this other document from the Company, which spells out its own position regarding conditions inside the Copper Cliff smelter."

At this McSorley-Winston frowned. "What? Harry, I really don't see the point—oh, very well."

Wardell began to grin as McSorley-Winston began to read. "Notice anything familiar, *Reg?*"

At first the Minister was silent as he read the Inco letter, but then, almost despite himself, he began to look back and forth between the two documents. As Wardell's point sank in, McSorley-Winston's neck began to redden just above his necktie. Soon the flush had risen to his face. "Well, yes, I do see a certain similarity here, but, so wh—"

"*Similarity?*" Wardell thundered, cutting McSorley-Winston off. "*They're bloody well the same!* You know that and I know that. You signed off on Inco's own appraisal of its own affairs! The very workplace you're supposed to be inspecting, that you're standing up in the House and telling the people of this province that you're regulating on their behalf, you let the company hacks in Copper Cliff write your own press release, don't change a word, not one comma, and you expect anyone to believe there's an honest, arm's length relationship here? *You're right in the Company's pocket, Reg, and this proves it! Dead to rights!*"

Wardell lowered his voice. "You know it, and I know it, Reg, but no on else has to."

McSorley-Winston's face had turned a beet red.

"But, but," he sputtered, "you don't mean—" he stood up tall to confront Wardell, a shorter man struggling to regain both his stature and his dignity. "Why Harry, that's blackmail! *You!* Threatening *me,* a Minister of the Crown?? Really, Harry, I had thought much better of you."

"Why you arrogant little son-of-a-bitch!" Wardell was in McSorley-Winston's face now, spittle flying, startling the smaller man with such vehemence at such close quarters. "*My* constituents spend eight hours a day in that shit hole, eating that dust and breathing that gas to the point they even start bleeding from their mouths and noses! You reassured the House, the news media, anyone who'd listen you had this file well in hand! What an embarrassment to you, to the whole government, *even to the Premier,* if this ever got out."

Wardell paused to let his words sink in. For his part McSorley-Winston was scrambling for cover, but there was none. Wardell was right. His own political future, his dream of a Party leadership bid when the Old Man stepped down that would make him— should he win, of course—Premier-designate of Ontario almost overnight, the Right Honourable

Reginald McSorley-Winston, it had such a ring! Why, the thing would love to happen—and now this. The Tory Minister's shoulders sagged, and he heaved a sigh of resignation. "All right, Wardell, what do you want?"

Harry smiled at the realization that he and the Minister of Natural Resources were, it seemed, no longer on a first name basis. He held up the forefinger of his right hand. "All right. First, the government introduces stringent annualized maximum atmospheric emission levels for SO_2."

He held up another finger. "Second, the Ministry sets up round-the-clock monitoring stations for ambient air quality *and especially SO_2* at the following locations in my riding." Wardell began enumerating with the remaining fingers of his right hand for emphasis. "One, the Pearl Street water tower, two, the Regent Street water tower, SO_2 levels not to exceed certain clearly stated and agreed to parts per million, any and all violations punishable by law."

McSorley-Winston nodded hypnotically at each of Wardell's points. Wouldn't this uncouth baboon ever run out of fingers? Even if he did, the Ontario Minister of Natural Resources half expected this loutish northern upstart to remove his shoes and socks to begin counting on his toes.

"Three," Harry continued happily, "a continuous atmospheric monitoring station to be established on the roof of the Post Office building, corner of Elm and Durham Streets, downtown Sudbury."

"Four . . ."

PART THREE

Epilogue

14

All the Way to Sweden

Within seventy-two months of Harry Wardell's confrontation with Reginald McSorley-Winston the Conservative-led government of Ontario introduced legislation stringently limiting atmospheric sulphur dioxide emissions in the province.

The legislation included establishment of continuous sulphur dioxide monitoring stations in and around downtown Sudbury.

Inco struggled to comply with mandated ground-level sulphur dioxide concentration limits in the Sudbury area, and, in the early 1970s, began construction of a huge smokestack to waft the toxic smelter fumes well away from the Nickel Capital.

The gigantic one-thousand-two-hundred-fifty-foot-high smokestack, soon dubbed "the superstack," was opposed by the Research Committee of Steelworkers Local 6500, which argued that it did nothing to solve the ultimate problem: industrial air pollution.

The superstack did, however, function as intended, protecting Sudbury and its residents from sulphur dioxide air pollution. The sulphur plume from the superstack was traced as far away as Sweden, and it was soon blamed for creating "acid rain," which led to the acidification of many lakes in Ontario's Muskoka region, a recreational area prized by many members of Ontario's elite, including the Premier and Frank Blaney, Managing Editor of *The Globe and Mail.*

Soon pinpointed as the largest single source of sulphur dioxide emissions in the Western Hemisphere, the superstack, and Inco's Copper Cliff smelter, quickly became an issue in U.S.-Canada negotiations to resolve the growing problem of acid rain, which threatened freshwater lakes in both countries.

In the early 1980s then-U.S. President Ronald Reagan and then-Canadian Prime Minister Brian Mulroney signed a bilateral agreement severely curtailing the air pollutants that caused acid rain.

As the result of the treaty, acid rain was attenuated, and lake acidification was reversed. Many see the acid rain treaty as a template for a potential global agreement on climate change in the twenty-first century.

In Sudbury the superstack, along with an aggressive effort to neutralize soil acidification, has resulted in the city earning global renown as a leader in healing industrially-damaged landscapes. The city's "lunar landscape" is no more.

Acclaimed Canadian author Margaret Atwood, a frequent visitor to Sudbury, now cites the city as a living example of the potential of human agency to combat such seemingly intractable environmental problems as climate change. "You should see what they've done in Sudbury," she tells audiences all over

the world. "If they can do it there we can do it anywhere. . ."

Harry Wardell went on to win five successive elections in Sudbury. . .

15

"$2.95 & Bus Fare"

. . .Harry Wardell gauged the mood of the crowd, the sea of expectant, upturned faces that awaited his words as he strode to the podium on the stage of the main auditorium of the Sudbury Steelworkers' Hall.

Fully nine years had passed since his victory, virtually unheard of for a freshman backbencher, over both Inco and the ruling Tories, in the fight for cleaner air in the province. The day he had quietly but unobtrusively stood in his place to vote "Aye!" for the Torys' Clean Air Act, grinning broadly at an ashen-faced Reginald McSorley-Winston, had been one of the happiest of his life.

But now another crisis—which had precipitated this monstrous Sudbury rally—loomed. Just days before Inco had shocked the world with its announcement that, healthy profits in 1975 and '76 notwithstanding, it would lay off thousands of its Sudbury workers in February 1978. Or rather new Steelworker Local 6500 President Jordan Nelson had made the announcement, upstaging Inco's own carefully planned news release. The move was typical of Nelson, a youthful, brash new breed of union leader—the first of the "young guys" to rise to power in the big Steelworkers Sudbury Local. Nelson's move to pre-empt Inco's press conference with one of his own hours earlier had proved highly controversial at the Union Hall, where he was roundly condemned "on the third floor," where the International Union maintained offices for its Staff Representatives, generally older union veterans who had moved up through the elected Local Union ranks into permanent full-time positions on the union payroll. "A union leader doesn't deliver the company's bad news, the company does," they had advised Nelson in no uncertain terms. But Nelson persisted, deftly stealing the march on the company. His audacity did not pass unnoticed, or unadmired, by the press corps, including Foley Gilpin, that crammed the Union Hall that memorable Friday morning. Commingling with the reporters, photographers and cameramen were a clutch of union officials, including Jake McCool, newly-elected Vice President of Local 6500, whose own meteoric rise up the hierarchy of the big Local rivalled Nelson's own.

And now both men were on the floor of the Steel Hall, watching Wardell's loping advance toward the podium. It had been an unforgettable seven days in Sudbury since Nelson's presser. His gloomy prognostication had indeed come to pass, with sensational—and immediate—fallout. Nothing like it had ever happened before in Canada—a financially healthy, profitable company suddenly deciding to idle a good chunk of its workforce! All during the week the Nickel City was a magnet to television news crews from all the major networks. Pundits and politicos scrambled to make sense of it all, and the "Inco lay-offs story" led the CBC's nightly television newscast three nights running. Even Foley Gilpin had been asked to venture his opinion. As a long-time Sud-burian, he found it impossible not to reflect the pro-found sense of doom that pervaded his hometown that early autumn. A company that had, for genera-tions, offered the promise of well-paid, steady employment for a lifetime was suddenly, for no apparent reason, tearing up that agreement with its home community, with its country. Where would it all end? It seemed a fine madness, aberrant behaviour with no bottom. The economic impact, Gilpin had predicted darkly in his gloomy op-ed, would soon be felt on the city's downtown streets, where abandoned storefronts would begin to dot the streets "like a rub-bie's gap-toothed grin."

A numbed sense of loss soon turned to downright anger. The "Nickel Capital of the World" had long since become accustomed to the vagaries of the boom-and-bust cycle of world metal markets, but this, this was different. The Americans' war in Vietnam, which had run up nickel prices for the pre-vious decade or more had ended, it was true, but com-modity prices had remained buoyant, and, so, too, had company profits. Howls of outrage filled the mouths of politicians and union leaders. A small air-plane buzzed in circles over downtown Sudbury, trailing a banner that read NATIONALIZE INCO.

The whole matter was coming to a climax now, as a thousand angry nickel workers shifted impatiently in their seats at the Steel Hall, pissed off and ugly, but eager to hear what their firebrand political representative Harry Wardell was about to say.

As he approached the podium on the stage high above the restless throng, Harry Wardell knew that he was treading with caution along two parallel political fault lines. There was, first of all, the question of nationalization. An increasingly popular notion since the announcement of the layoffs, the position of a government takeover was tempered by the memory of recent events in Chile, where a democratically-elected but leftist President, Salvador Allende, had expropriated the American-owned copper mines in his country. The move triggered a wave of bloody, anti-government violence and Allende perished in a hail of bullets inside his own Presidential Palace. The resulting coup ushered in a decade of brutal fascistic repression led by the Chilean military. Many observers believed the coup had been encouraged and secretly funded by the U.S. Central Intelligence Agency, a claim that was sombrely and flatly denied by no less a personage than Secretary of State Henry Kissinger.

Still, the Chilean events stood as an object lesson to any political leaders who dared tamper with American-owned interests in their own countries. Certainly, the lesson was not lost on Ontario's political leaders who, at least in Harry's estimation, were so buddy-buddy and beholden to International Nickel as to make declarations calling for nationalization just so much empty rhetoric which might play well with this crowd but would, in fact, accomplish very little.

Even still, the leader of Harry's own party, a man long noted for his rhetorical brilliance, had adopted a cautious position when he'd spoken earlier, stopping just short of calling for nationalization outright, though he'd done so with typical hortatory flourish. "When a corporation shoots an arrow through the heart of a community," he had declared grandly, "then we must take away its corporate bow!" His grandiloquence had served only to lower the room temperature from the boiling point to tepid, and was greeted by polite applause.

The second fault line, Harry recognized, was the issue of compensation. How much should Inco's Wall Street owners be paid in the highly unlikely event that McSorley-Winston and his cronies actually ever moved against Inco? The hard-line position here was that Inco shareholders had already been amply compensated by the billions of dollars plundered from the rich Sudbury mines over the previous century. On the other hand, it was true that American investors had been willing to risk millions to open the Sudbury mining camp at a time when no Canadian investors were willing or able to follow suit. . .

How would he come down on the question of first, nationalization, and then of compensation?

It is possible that even Harry himself does not know the answer as he steps to the podium this Sunday afternoon with the TV cameras from all the big national news networks rolling, their glass eyes pointing at him from atop their tripods way at the back of the big room as Harry bends his long, lean frame over the podium, pausing to adjust the microphone just so, so that it will deliver his rich baritone perfectly to the expectant throng down below that stretches back to the far corners of the big room, so far that exact details are lost in a haze of commingled cigarette smoke and angry popular blue funk.

As Harry leans in above the crowd, his forearms resting atop the angled podium, a dark suit-clad figure newly arrived from the Holy Mount, he begins to speak, and his words take flight, soaring above the thousand rough-hewn faces, hungry for truth, for emotion, for *justice* oh Jesus just once in this life of drill, blast, of drill again, please Jesus just this once give us *justice*!

And he feels it, Harry feels this terrible, flaming thirst for justice and is swept up in it, and is borne aloft, "and so I say 'Hell yes, let's take over these goddamned bastards!'" Harry pauses, and smiles approvingly at the roar of approbation that rises from a thousand parched and fevered throats. But the roar is sustained and it breaks in on itself like some terrible, ineluctable wave. At last Harry signals for silence so he can continue. "And when people ask me 'Should we compensate the Company?' My answer is 'Yes, we should compensate the Company, *and pay them every penny we owe them*! And you know how much that is, don'cha?" Harry pauses here for a beat, hunched still more over the podium, leaning in even further, and an unaccustomed silence falls over the crowd waiting, expectant, for Harry's answer. "*Two ninety five and bus fare!"* Harry stretches out one long arm, his index finger twitching, pointing south, toward Toronto, toward the way out of town.

Another split second of silence elapses as Harry's words and gesture sinks in, but once it has a deafening thunderclap of rapture and joy erupts from the crowd and they are on their feet now, stamping the wooden floor with their work boots, and the tumult is fine and they can see it now, a future without white hats hovering, telling them needlessly what to do next and the noise threatens to lift the roof of the Steelworkers' Hall from its moorings, a roaring that rivals even the rolling concussive booming of the blasts underground, and it is Sunday and they will live forever and the words of their roaring will roll out from Frood Road to the far corners of the camp, all the way out to crest in Levack and then roll back again, and there is no hint, no intimation of the terrible time of testing that lies dead ahead.

. . . Introducing

Part Three of "The Nickel Range Trilogy"; an exclusive preview of the final, concluding novel in the series in Mick Lowe's sweeping chronicle of life in the "Nickel Capital of the World," and of the epic struggle for control of the fabulous riches buried deep beneath the city's streets, *Year of the Long Strike*:

Year of the Long Strike

"Revolution is the workers' festival."
V.I. Lenin

Like all good movies, this one begins with a song.

It was everywhere that fall and late summer of 1978, rattling out of the tinny speakers of cheap transistor radios in truck-stop kitchens, booming out of two-ton Wurlitzer jukebox woofers in every honkytonk bar north of the French, always sung with a Nashville twang coarse and unadorned as a rasp file: *Take this job and shove it! I ain't workin' here no more!*

It was seen by all of them as *their* song, telling the story of their lives, their theme song. And they would, in their thousands, have flipped the company the bird as they strode through the plant gates that end-of-shift, except both hands were full, as they lugged their belongings and dirty laundry from cleaned out lockers.

A total of more than eleven thousand hardrock miners and nickel smelter and refinery workers left the plants with swagger that afternoon: *Take this job and shove it!* They were pulling the pin, stickin' it to the Man. Greeting their departing comrades brimming with a bravado their wives might not have shared, thinking of their children with no Christmas, and cash running low over the long winter months ahead: "Out 'til the grass is green, brother!"

"Fuckin' A! Out 'til the grass is green!"

They were like lemmings, piling off a high cliff, about to plunge to their own mass graves, all the papers and politicians said so, even the political leaders of their own, social democratic party, the party of the workers. Hell, even some of their own union leaders said it: "Do Not Strike: Union Leader" was the headline blazoned page one above the fold in the province's largest circulation daily newspaper.

And they all knew it was true: they were taking on a powerful and enormously rich opponent, one they had strengthened by letting their own stupidity and cupidity crowd out common sense by creating a huge stockpile—enough to last the company a year without an ounce of additional production—in their eagerness to make money through overtime work and the bonus system.

So maybe they *were* like men waiting for the trap door to swing. Fuck it! They were young, many of them, and they were cocky. *Take this job and shove it! I ain't workin' here no more!*

Out 'til the grass is green, brother!

Out 'til the grass is green!

Afterword
and Acknowledgements

I must, first of all, give due credit for the title of this book to a legendary former Sudburian who is not, alas, alive to read these words. Some forty years have now passed since I first read the phrase "feeding the insatiable maw of the Copper Cliff smelter" as being the *raison d'etre* for Sudbury's mines and its miners--if not for the whole city itself—in an op-ed column penned by the late Elmer Sopha. The phrase jumped out at me at the time, and it has stayed with me ever since.

Lawyer, legislator, genius orator, journalist *manqué* (he once confided to me that, if he had it to do all over again he thought he'd become a reporter) Elmer was *sui generis,* a true Sudbury original, but also, it must be said, a deeply flawed and troubled—even tragic—public figure who towered over the rest of us. His ineffable sadness, which led him to so much self-destructive behaviour, licked him in the end, and I am happy to revive his memory here, however briefly.

And then there is an entire supporting cast of living Sudburians who have appeared to share their memories of the epic true-life battle upon which this story was based. Elie Martel, Norris Valiquette, and David Patterson were invaluable in this regard, as was the late Homer Seguin, whose constant re-telling of this story over the decades kept its memory alive. I received invaluable technical advice and assistance about the smelter and its myriad processes from Norris and from Jamie West. Any factual or technical errors in the text are my own.

To a considerable degree *The Maw* owes its very existence to the financial success of its predecessor, Volume One of *The Nickel Range Trilogy, The Raids,* for which I must once again thank the usual suspects: Robin Philpot of Baraka Books in Montreal, my long-time agent, Janine Cheeseman, of Aurora Artists in Toronto, and the members of my crack mini-marketing team: Ian MacDonald, Julia Lowe and Melanie Lowe. You kids are all right.

And yes, the quotations in the final chapter of this novel are excerpted, verbatim, from the actual document that so incriminated the then-governing party of Ontario in its dealings with Inco that the last, best face-saving measure was to pass the sweeping clean-air legislation that forced the clean-up of the Copper Cliff smelter, a technically-challenging, multi-billion-dollar task that continues even today, in 2014.

It was not the first, not the last, time in the history of the Canadian nickel industry that powerful interests would do the right thing for the wrong reason, as the reader will soon see . . .

Publisher's Note –
Follow-up to *The Raids*

We launched *The Raids*, volume 1 of *The Nickel Range Trilogy*, before a crowd of some sixty friends and supporters at the Steelworkers' Hall in Sudbury on May 25, 2014. At the same time Oryst Sawchuk, who illustrated both *The Raids* and *The Insatiable Maw*, inaugurated the Mining Art Exhibition of his work at Gallery 6500 in the Steelworkers' Hall. (Mick Lowe was elected founding chairman of the Gallery 6500 board.) Borrowing from Pablo Neruda, Oryst described the exhibition as a tribute "to those who have penetrated the bowels of the Earth" and an honour to the memories of miners killed on the job.

Quite coincidentally, Jack Pauzé, an eighty-nine-year-old former constable, attended the launch and brought original 1960s clippings from *The Sudbury Daily Star* following the real siege of the Mine Mill Hall in August 1961 and another with a huge ad that appeared in January 1962.

For the record, we are pleased to reproduce some parts of the clippings that Jack Pauzé kept so carefully all these years. They illustrate the veracity of the story told in *The Raids* and the international character of the events.

Front Page of *Sudbury Star* on Monday, August 28, 1961 after occupation of the Mine Mill Hall on Regent Street.

HUNDREDS IN INFLAMED CROWDS OUTSIDE UNION HALL WERE NON-UNION MEMBERS 'OUT FOR KICKS' BUT NO HELP TO LAW AND ORDER
Deputy Chief Bert Guillet, in charge of police squad that did fine job, urges restraint, warns against rough-house tactics

Sudbury Star: "Hundreds in inflamed crowds outside union hall were non-union members 'out for kicks' but no help to law and order; Deputy Chief Bert Guillet, in charge of police squad that did fine job, urges restraint, warns against rough-house tactics."

In *The Raids*, Oryst Sawchuk illustrated the siege Mick Lowe describes which resembles the one reported in the *Sudbury Star*.

Star Cameras Catch

A TOUGH TANGLE FOR 'INVADERS' TO BREAK THROUGH
Door barricaded with mound of chairs by Kennedy forces

"Okay, now! Everybody push now! Aaaand hard!
Harder! Aaand now! One more time, boys! Give 'er
shit like nice!" But it was no use. The harder they
pushed, the stouter the resistance became. Just as
Big Bill had foreseen, the jumble of stacking chairs
tangled against the door at the bottom of the
staircase inside settled into a solid mass the more
force was applied against them from outside.
(*The Raids* p. 212)

Full-page ad in *The Sudbury Star* on January 24, 1962 (page 8). All the stops were pulled to convince workers to leave the Mine Mill Union and complete "the raid."

This ad shows, as did Mick Lowe in *The Raids,* that the battles in Sudbury's mines and streets in the 1960s were simply the epicenter of the Cold War in North America. Though the story takes place in Sudbury, it could also be Trail, B.C., Thompson, Manitoba, Port Colborne, Ontario, or any number of mining towns in the United States.